COUNTDOWN TO DISASTER

300 MINUTES OF DANGER

JACK HEATH

STERLING CHILDREN'S BOOKS
New York

For Clare Forster, without whom I couldn't be a writer -J. H.

STERLING CHILDREN'S BOOKS
New York

An Imprint of Sterling Publishing Co., Inc.
1166 Avenue of the Americas
New York, NY 10036

STERLING CHILDREN'S BOOKS and the distinctive Sterling Children's Books logo are registered trademarks of Sterling Publishing Co., Inc.

Text © 2015 Jack Heath
Interior illustration © 2015 Scholastic Australia
Cover © 2020 Sterling Publishing Co., Inc.

Previously published by Scholastic Australia in 2015, 2017

ISBN 978-1-4549-3141-6

Library of Congress Cataloging-in-Publication Data

Names: Heath, Jack, 1986- author.
Title: 300 minutes of danger / Jack Heath.
Other titles: Three hundred minutes of danger
Description: New York : Sterling Children's Books, [2020] | Series:
  Countdown to disaster ; 1 | "Previously published by Scholastic
  Australia 2015, 2017." | Audience: Ages 10-13. | Summary: "George is
  trapped in a falling airplane with no engine or pilot. Milla is covered
  in radioactive waste-and her hazmat suit is running out of air. Otto is
  in the depths of the ocean, where something hungry is circling. Ten
  linked stories. Ten life-or-death situations. Ten brave kids. Each drama
  takes 30 minutes to play out-and kids get to read it in real time!*"--
  Provided by publisher.
Identifiers: LCCN 2019041300 | ISBN 9781454931416 (trade paperback) | ISBN
  9781454938415 (epub)
Subjects: CYAC: Survival--Fiction.
Classification: LCC PZ7.H3478 Aam 2020 | DDC [Fic]--dc23
LC record available at https://lccn.loc.gov/2019041300

Distributed in Canada by Sterling Publishing Co., Inc.
c/o Canadian Manda Group, 664 Annette Street
Toronto, Ontario M6S 2C8, Canada

For information about custom editions, special sales, and premium and corporate purchases, please contact Sterling Special Sales at 800-805-5489 or specialsales@sterlingpublishing.com.

Manufactured in Canada

Lot #:
2 4 6 8 10 9 7 5 3 1
03/20

sterlingpublishing.com

Design by Julie Robine

Additional illustration credits
iStockphoto.com; Grunge Border © Rochakred | Dreamstime.com; mountain icon © AnnaFrajtova | iStockphoto.com; submarine icon © AnsyAgeeva | iStockphoto.com; nuclear, snowflake, temperature and poison icons © Ecelop |iStockphoto.com; diamond icon © nkuchumova | iStockphoto.com; syringe icon © nadyaillyustrator | iStockphoto.com; train icon © Jacartoon | iStockphoto.com; rocket icon © istrejman | iStockphoto.com

CONTENTS

BOARDING SCHOOL

"**W**e're flying really low," George said. "Are we going to make it over those mountains?"

The pilot laughed. "Of course! Don't worry."

His confidence made George worry more rather than less. The Russian wilderness stretched out to the horizon in every direction, miles of ice and skeletal black trees. He couldn't see any towns through the dirty window. There weren't even any roads. Russia was the biggest country in the world, which meant a lot of empty space. He and the pilot might be the only two people within fifty miles or more.

The pilot was a Finnish man who spoke impeccable English and was as pale as a vampire. He had only one hand on the steering wheel while the other fiddled with his silver earring. His legs were crossed, and a half-empty can of soda was balanced next to the throttle. He didn't seem to be taking his job very seriously.

On commercial flights, pilots usually made boring speeches about weather patterns and arrival times.

30:00

29:30

28:50

01

Now George understood why. Blasting along 3,000 miles above the ground at almost 200 miles per hour, it was hard to feel safe with a pilot who had a personality. Passengers wanted to believe the person in charge was essentially a robot. No sense of humor, no new ideas, no mistakes.

27:30 But today the illusion wasn't there. The plane had no barrier between the cabin and the cockpit. There were only two people on board: George and the pilot.

The Ural mountain range was still a long way off, but it looked lethal. The sun was rising behind the jagged peaks, capped with spikes of ice. It was as though the horizon were lined with shark teeth.

George told himself not to worry. After all, the mountains were the point of the trip. No use taking a snowboard to a completely flat landscape. And as for the pilot, well, he probably knew what he was doing.

27:20 Technically the snowboarding camp—"boarding school," George called it—didn't start until next week. George's parents had come to Russia early so they could do some kind of work for the department of agriculture. George had begged them to let him spend a few days practicing in the Urals. Had they met the pilot, they would never have agreed.

27:00 *We won't crash,* George told himself. *That hardly ever happens in real life.*

The inside of the plane was tiny, with only six furry seats and a ceiling too low for George to stand up properly. It felt like traveling in a minibus on a dirt road. According to George's sister, whose grades in math and science were spectacular, some pockets of air were denser than others. This made the plane bounce around like a dinghy on the high seas.

George didn't understand the physics—*shouldn't air just be air*? He was better with languages, like German and French.

"My cousin," the pilot said, yelling to be heard over the engine. "He owns the finest hotel in Novosibirsk. You should stay with him."

25:00

"Thank you," George said, "but my hotel is already booked."

"Believe me," the pilot said, conversely making George believe him less, "it will be worth the cancelation fee." He picked at something in his teeth, neither hand on the steering wheel now.

"My parents made the reservation," George said. "They're waiting for me there."

24:30

He looked out the window just in time to see something fall from the sky. It was round and shiny, like a bowling ball or a motorcycle helmet. But before George could get a good look at it—

It was sucked into the engine.

Boom!

The plane lurched sideways.

The seatbelt bit into George's hips, and the soda can flew off its perch. Panic lit up the pilot's face as he swore in Finnish and grabbed the steering wheel. Warning lights blinked all over the cockpit.

23:30 Oxygen masks fell from hidden compartments above about half of the seats. The compartment above George's head sprang open but nothing fell out. The mask must have been lost or damaged.

After pushing the left throttle all the way forward and pulling the right all the way back, the pilot got the plane under control. The horizon leveled out, and George's heart rate slowed back down to somewhere near normal.

22:15 "What was that?" he demanded.

"It wasn't my fault," the pilot said. "Something hit us. A bird, perhaps."

"No, it was round. It fell from somewhere above us."

"Space debris, maybe." He tapped a dial that looked like the speedometer in George's mom's car. The needle was easing downward. "I had to divert the power away from the damaged engine to prevent fire. We're losing altitude."

21:50 The spikes of the Ural mountain range didn't look so distant anymore. "Will we still clear the

04

mountains?" George asked.

21:00

"One minute." The pilot grabbed a notepad and pencil and scratched out some calculations. George held his breath. Weren't they supposed to use computers for this sort of thing?

"Yes," the pilot said finally. "We'll pass over them with sixty-eight feet to spare. See? I told you not to worry."

George stared at him. Sixty-eight feet didn't sound like much room for error.

"Is there a landing strip somewhere?" George asked.

"Yes. To the north."

19:30

The pilot turned the steering wheel and did something with the pedals beneath his feet. The plane banked sideways. A sick rumbling echoed from the remaining engine. The wings rattled like an unbalanced washing machine, and the plane swooped downward. The pilot twisted the wheel back hurriedly and the plane righted itself.

19:00

"The rudder has been damaged," he said. "We can't turn or we'll lose too much altitude. Now we only have . . ." He scribbled out another calculation. ". . . twenty-nine feet of clearance. If we try to steer toward the landing strip, we'll crash into the mountains."

George's stomach hurt. Even for an extreme-sport

enthusiast, this was too much.

"If we can't turn," he said, "then what are we going to land on?"

The pilot was already grabbing a tattered map and a ruler. George could make out a few names of cities, or maybe provinces—Kyshtym, Kasli, Argayash. The pilot marked their current coordinates. A few seconds later he did it again. Then he used the two points to extrapolate, drawing a line along the ruler to—

"Oh no," he muttered. His face had gone even paler than before. "No, no!"

"What is it?" George demanded.

The pilot flicked a few switches, got out of his chair and started moving to the back of the plane.

"What are we going to hit?" George demanded again. "Another mountain?"

"Much worse," the pilot said. "We're going to have to evacuate."

"Evacuate? As in—"

The pilot was already pulling on a backpack marked PARACHUTE. George's physics may not have been good, but he was top of his class in French. *Protection contre la chute* meant *protect from falling.*

"We're going to jump out of the plane?" George felt dizzy.

"Trust me," the pilot said. "It's better than the

06

alternative."

He approached the emergency exit door, grabbed the handle and wrenched it downward. The door exploded out into the void so fast that it was like a magic trick. George's ears popped and he stumbled sideways as the plane rocked. The roaring of the wind was deafening. The cold blowing off the peaks of the Ural mountains turned his veins to ice.

This was all wrong. "I don't know how to use a parachute!" George cried.

16:00

"It's easy. Just pull the ripcord ten seconds after you jump." The pilot didn't even look at George as he turned to the open doorway and threw himself out. He was sucked away instantly, leaving George alone in a crippled plane en route to who-knew-what.

15:30

George rummaged in the closet the pilot's parachute had come from. There was only one more. When he picked it up it felt too light to save his life. But he guessed that was the point. The chute would be made of fibers strong enough to hold him up but not heavy enough to drag him down.

15:00

He pulled the chute onto his back.

One of the shoulder straps snapped.

George stared at the torn fabric, alarmed. Perhaps he could tie a knot in it, but he wouldn't know if it would take his weight until he pulled the ripcord. And were those tooth marks?

He turned the parachute pack over and found a hole tunneled through the canvas. Surrounded by a cocoon of ripped nylon was a dead rat, its flaky skin stretched across its bones. It had made a nest in there before it starved to death.

14:30

George dropped the parachute with a yelp. It was useless. Had the pilot known only one of the chutes was usable? Was that why he had jumped out so quickly, instead of sticking around long enough to show George how it worked?

George ran to the open door. Just being so close to the sickening drop gave him vertigo. The drifts and valleys in the snow below looked like the divots in a misshapen golf ball. He gripped the safety rails with both hands. The ground was still at least half a mile away. If the parachute didn't work properly, there was no way he'd survive the fall.

14:00

His other option was to stay on board and attempt an emergency landing. But the pilot—a man with training and experience—had been so terrified of the terrain ahead that he'd thrown himself out of the plane rather than try to land it. What hope did George have?

13:40

He ran back to the cockpit. A radio dangled from the ceiling. He grabbed it and pressed the trigger in the side. "Hello?" he yelled. "My plane is going down and

I don't know how to fly it! Mayday, Mayday, Mayday!"

Another French word. *M'aider. Help me.*

13:10

There was only the hiss of static. George switched channels and tried again. Nothing. After trying five different channels with no response, he guessed the radio must be broken. No rudder, no radio, no para-chute—did anything in this stupid plane work?

The Ural mountains loomed in the windshield, rocky peaks glistening. George didn't have much confidence in the pilot's calculations. The plane might not even make it over the mountains. If he was going to jump out, he had to do it soon.

He knotted the broken strap, pulled the chute on, and ran back to the emergency exit. The snow below looked no closer. The heat from the remaining engine cut a shimmering trail through the air. As an extreme sportsman he knew that skydivers often broke their legs on landing. Even a fully functioning parachute could only slow a falling body so much. How much damage had the rat done?

But he had no choice.

11:30

George settled into a crouch, ready to hurl himself out the door—

Then he stood up. It was too scary.

He crouched again, telling himself that if he didn't jump, he would die—

And hesitated. Perhaps there was another way.

He looked out the front windows again. He had perhaps sixty seconds before the plane passed over the mountains, or crashed into them.

11:00 He yanked the overhead compartment open and tossed a bag aside, revealing his snowboard—a freeride board made from high-performance polyethylene with a strip of steel around the edge. It was too long for half-pipe riding or trick jumps, but maybe the size would save his life.

10:30 He ripped off his shoes, pulled on his boarding boots and strapped them into the bindings atop the board.

He pulled on his padded goggles, wishing he had a helmet too. If he hit his head on landing and blacked out, he could freeze to death before anyone found him.

09:55 He hopped over to the emergency exit, board scraping the floor. No time to take off the parachute—the mountain was right below him. The pilot's arithmetic had been correct after all. The snowy peak was only about twenty-five feet below the speeding plane.

Close enough. George took a deep breath and hurled himself out of the plane.

The stream of hot air blasting through the remaining engine blew him off course immediately. He spun like a toy on a string, the horizon whooshing

past him over and over as he tumbled toward the
mountain. He felt like he was going to throw up.

09:20

He stretched his arms and legs out, fighting for
balance. The air pounded his clothes, as if he were
wrapped in a blanket while a group of boxing champ-
ions hit him with gloved fists, but soon he was
right-side up.

Just in time. George slammed into the snow with
an incredible amount of force, not so much from the
plane's height as its speed. Twin shocks spiraled up his
legs and suddenly he was rocketing down the slope,
his board carving a trail in the snow.

08:00

"Woooohooooo!" he screamed as he zoomed across
the white powder, faster than he had ever gone before.
The plane shot past above him, rumbling away into the
distance. Soon it disappeared over the next peak.
Perhaps he would never know where it would end up.
But he was alive.

For now. George turned back to the slope and saw
for the first time where he was headed.

07:20

His jaw dropped. A crevasse lay between the two
mountains—a wide, deep chasm with smooth, ice-
blue walls stretching down into darkness. Soon he
would plunge in.

He twisted his board sideways, trying to stop, but
the slope was steep and he was sliding too fast. The

snow had turned to ice beneath his board. He had to spin back the right way to avoid losing his balance. He couldn't stop, and he couldn't steer around it.

Perhaps he could jump over it.

06:30 George crouched, reducing the wind resistance and getting closer to the board. It skittered faster and faster across the ice. The crevasse yawned up ahead. This was a mistake. The closer he got, the wider it looked—and deeper. He was almost at the edge and he still couldn't see the bottom. If he didn't make the jump, he would fall to his death.

But he had to try. There was nothing else he could do. He was a prisoner of his earlier choices.

He swept closer and closer to the edge—

And jumped.

06:00 Gravity disappeared. The snow vanished out from under the board, leaving George to stare down into a pit so dark it looked endless. The walls were a brutally sharp patchwork of ice and stone.

He hurtled toward the far side, the sun glinting off the steel rim of his board, snow trailing behind it like a jet stream.

But he was too heavy. His velocity was slipping away. Halfway across the crevasse he could already tell he wasn't going to make it. He was falling too fast.

05:50 If he was lucky, he would crash into the stone wall on the other side of the chasm and be killed on impact. If he was unlucky, he would fall deeper and deeper, accelerating into the frozen shadows below before he was eventually crushed against the bottom of the chasm. No one would ever find his body. His parents and his sister would never know what had happened to him. And all because of a ruined parachute.

His parachute!

05:40

George grabbed the ripcord and yanked it. The nylon parachute exploded out of his pack with a sound like a cardboard box being crushed by a speeding semitrailer. George plummeted as the chute burst into shape above him, shredded by the rat's teeth. The knotted straps of the backpack dug into his shoulders and across his chest.

The parachute actually seemed to *scream* as the wind whistled through all the gaping holes in the fabric above him. It was hopeless. There was no way it would slow him down enough to survive the impact. All he had done was give himself a burial shroud.

04:30

Snap! George's head jerked forward and his arms nearly popped out of their sockets as the ropes went taut. His legs kicked wildly in the void, held a set distance apart by the snowboard. His breaths reverberated around the cavern. He still couldn't see the bottom of the crevasse, but somehow he had stopped falling. What had happened?

He looked up. One of the holes in the chute was snagged on the jagged edge of the cliff. Now he was hanging from the ropes that connected his pack to the chute.

He laughed, his voice bouncing crazily between the walls of the crevasse as the adrenaline thinned out in his system and his heart slowed down from a sprint to a jog. By chewing that hole in the chute, the dead rat had saved his life.

03:00 *Rrrrrrip.*

It almost sounded like a growling dog—a little Chihuahua or a Pomeranian. George looked up in horror. He hadn't imagined it.

The chute was tearing.

Rrrip.

02:41 As he watched, the hole in the nylon got a little wider. It was too damaged to support his weight.

No time to waste. The cliff face was out of reach and there were no handholds anyway. Instead, George grabbed the ropes and started dragging himself up, hand over hand.

02:20 This increased the strain on the chute. The tear spread faster across the nylon. Soon the last few fibers would snap, sending George tumbling down into the crevasse.

He hauled himself up as fast as he dared. He kept his eyes on the gray sky as though that would make him weightless.

`02:00`

Every handhold took him closer to the top of the cliff, but it also widened the tear. For every few feet he climbed, he lost almost half as much. His lungs ached from sucking in the freezing air. The muscles in his arms burned. His snowboard felt terrifyingly heavy beneath him, but he couldn't spare a hand to remove it.

When he was almost at the top, the last threads of the chute snapped. The cliff edge sheared through them like a guillotine through tissue paper.

George felt himself begin to fall. He flung out a desperate hand—

`01:40`

And caught the edge of the cliff.

The chute fell down on top of him like a drop cloth over a priceless statue. He swiped it off with his free hand and then grabbed the cold stone, mashing the pads of his fingertips against his bones. Knowing his luck, the cliff would begin to crumble any second now. He clawed at the ice, hauling himself up onto it, elbow, elbow, knee, knee. Then he crawled a safe distance from the edge and collapsed.

`01:00`

He lay there for a moment, the snow burning his cheek. The only sound was the distant whispering of the wind as it swept over the Siberian wilderness. The sun emerged from behind a cloud.

The plane took off about twenty minutes before George jumped out, and flew at roughly 200 miles per hour. That made him more than 50 miles from civilization. He had no food, no shelter and no way to contact the rest of the world.

00:30

Luckily, most of his journey would be downhill.

George detached his boots from the binders on the board and clambered to his feet. He used his shadow to work out which way west was, then he put his board under his arm and started sloshing through the snow toward the top of the next peak.

00:00

His adventure was only just beginning.

SUB-HUMAN

"Once you're at the bottom of the ocean, grab any- 30:00 thing you can find," Otto's mother said. "The weirder the better."

"I don't understand." Otto gripped the safety rail and peered over the edge into the roiling sea. "If the virus comes from flies, why would the cure be on the seabed?"

Mom ignored him. "How's it going?" she called to the engineer.

"Getting there." The engineer was fiddling with the hatch of the neon-green submersible in a way that Otto didn't find reassuring. He half hoped the engineer wouldn't be able to get it open. 29:30

Then Otto wouldn't have to go down into the black.

A cloud cast a shadow across the ship. The salty breeze whipped at Otto's hair. A sliver of land was still visible on the horizon. He knew how bad it was back there—hundreds dead, thousands barricaded inside their homes, hospitals overflowing—but it couldn't be nearly as scary as where he was going.

28:45

"The virus doesn't come from flies," Mom said. It took Otto a moment to realize she was speaking to him. "Flies just carry it. Genetic tags tell us the virus came from the trench below us. But according to the sonar, there's a huge amount of movement down there, which means life forms must have developed an immunity, or else the virus would have wiped them out. If we can study them, we can probably cure it."

"If there's so much life down there," Otto said, "how come we haven't studied it before?"

"We know more about the surface of the moon than the bottom of the sea," Mom said. "It's really hard to get to the ocean floor because of the pressure, and once you're down there, it's really hard to see."

28:00

Otto looked at the submersible. Giant halogen floodlights were mounted on the sides. "What about those?"

"Even with the lights on, you won't be able to see much," Mom said. "The water is full of dirt stirred up by the currents, and those lamps only create wavelengths of light that are invisible to most fish. We don't want to scare anything off."

27:40

Currents. Wavelengths. Life forms. How had Otto gotten himself into this?

The *Endeavour* had left port nine hours ago with a crew of fourteen. Otto, his mother, seven engineers, and five scientists. Then Chapman—a little man with a bristly mustache and a scar on his cheek—got sick. No one seemed sure exactly what he had, but it had something to do with his lungs, and was severe enough that he had to be quarantined in a little room on the port side of the vessel.

No one said out loud that Chapman might have the "flyrus." But Otto knew they were thinking it.

The neon-green submersible had been designed specifically for Chapman. But if he went down there while he was ill, the pressure could kill him. If they went back to land to pick up a new pilot, the worsening weather could make the dive impossible. And every hour they spent debating what to do, more people were falling prey to the virus sweeping the mainland.

The only other person on board small enough to fit in the submersible was Otto.

"Go back to the pressure," Otto said. "What do I do if it leaks?"

"The vessel is made from syntactic foam," the engineer said. "The more pressure there is, the stronger the material gets. So if there's a leak—"

"Which there won't be," Mom put in.

"It'll happen near the surface," the engineer continued. "So we'll just pull you back up."

"OK, so no leaks," Otto said. "But there's got to be a

27:00

25:50

25:00

limit to how much pressure it can take, right? What if it implodes?"

"That could happen," the engineer admitted. "But it was designed to withstand up to 114 MPa. At the bottom of this trench you should only be exposed to 110 MPa."

24:30

That didn't sound like much of a safety margin to Otto.

"But what if it *does* implode?" he pressed.

Mom and the engineer looked at one another.

"It won't," Mom said.

Her answer told Otto more than he wanted to know. He could only hope that if the massive pressure on the seabed crushed the submersible, it would happen fast. No fear, no pain—just the walls rushing in to kill him so quickly that he'd be dead before he knew he was in trouble.

For a moment he wished he had a normal mother. The sort who smiled and laughed and fussed over him and worried about him and didn't drag him along on crazy science expeditions. She had said he would be safer with her than on the mainland, but that had turned out to be false. He wished he had the sort of Mom who would tell him he didn't need to do this.

23:10

But he *did* have to. No one else could. So maybe he should be grateful that she wasn't trying to convince him he had a choice.

The vessel didn't look much like a submersible. It looked more like a lime-green cartridge, ready to be loaded into a giant printer. It was tall and thin, with what looked like tank treads attached to the bottom and two spindly robotic arms hanging from the sides. ▬22:40

"It's so tall," Otto said. "What if it tips over?"

"The top weighs less than the bottom," the engineer said. "If it falls over, it'll just stand itself back up again." He finally got the glass dome on top open, revealing a circular control panel around two dark holes. "OK! Good to go."

Otto clambered gingerly into the submersible. His legs slotted neatly into the two holes. There were pedals beneath his feet. ▬21:00

"The pedals control the treads," the engineer said, as if reading Otto's mind. "Tilt your feet forward to move forward. Tilt back to move back. Tilt your feet opposite ways to turn around."

Otto tried it. He could hear the treads whirring beneath him, but because the submersible was still suspended above the water, it didn't go anywhere.

"These two joysticks control the arms," the engineer continued. "When you find something worth picking up, pull the trigger and the hand will snap closed. If you've successfully grabbed it, push the green button. The hand will automatically put the object in the sample pouch. If you missed, push the red button. The hand will open and you can try again."

"What *is* worth picking up?" Otto asked.

"Anything alive," Mom said. "Or recently dead. Coral is good, fish is great. The bigger the better, and the more variety the better. But no rocks, no dirt. Those are worth studying, but today we have more important things to collect."

"There's a ballast attached to the bottom of the vessel," the engineer continued. "It'll weigh you down so you sink to the bottom. When you've filled all the sample pouches, hit these two switches. That will release the ballast so you float back up. The ballast is designed to dissolve within twenty-four hours of contact with saltwater, so even if the battery is damaged and you lose power, you won't have to worry about getting stuck down there."

19:10 It hadn't occurred to Otto to worry about that until the engineer mentioned it. He felt less safe rather than more—like when he saw a dog with a muzzle, or when the crash position was explained on an airplane.

"These controls here are for the radio—we've turned it on and preset the frequency, so don't touch them. Anything else you need to know?"

This was all happening too fast. Otto was so

overwhelmed that he couldn't think of any questions, but he had no doubt that as soon as the craft was underwater he would think of something he should have asked.

"OK then," the engineer said. He went to close the hatch, but Mom stopped him.

`18:00`

She leaned over Otto. "Good luck," she said, and kissed him on the cheek. That should have been comforting, but it was out of character for her. It reminded Otto of how much danger he was in.

"Thanks," he said.

The engineer closed the hatch. As the silence closed in, Otto remembered the question he should have asked—*how much air is in here?*

Plenty. Surely. There would be no point having a dissolving mechanism that let the pod float back up to the surface after twenty-four hours if there wasn't enough air to last that long.

Still, he found himself taking shallower breaths. His hands were clammy against the joysticks.

The radio fizzed and crackled. "Otto," the engineer said. "Can you hear me?"

`17:30`

"Loud and clear," Otto said.

"OK. We're going to—"

Snap! There was a sickening lurch. Otto found himself floating in the air for a second before the vessel slammed down into the ocean. He sprawled forward over the controls on impact.

Just as the engineer had promised, the sub didn't tip over. The ballast dragged it straight down.

"What happened?" Otto demanded.

"The cable snapped," the engineer said. "It was calibrated for Chapman. You must be heavier. You OK?"

Otto tried to stifle his dread as the water rose up the sides of the dome and then closed over the top of him. He couldn't see what was below. He could only look up and watch the rippling surface move farther and farther away.

"I'm fine," he lied. "But this means you can't pull me up. Right?"

"Right."

"What if there's a leak?"

"There won't be," the engineer promised.

16:20 The ocean was vast but not empty. A distant underwater mountain was encrusted with coral. A cloud of jellyfish pulsed around in lazy circles. Something bumped against the vessel, and Otto whirled around in time to see a receding tailfin.

"Shark!" he cried. "I've got sharks down here!"

"Don't worry," the engineer said. "Even a big shark couldn't bite through the synthetic foam. They'll be curious, but they can't hurt you."

Otto wondered why it was the engineer talking him through this. He would have preferred his mother, but he was too proud to say so.

By the time the shark turned back toward him, revealing a mouth of crooked fangs, Otto had already sunk out of its reach.

The deeper he descended, the darker the ocean became. Soon it was like being outside at night. After that, it was as if the dome had been painted black. The only light came from the glow of his instruments.

The vessel creaked ominously as more and more water moved in to crush it.

"The hull is making noises," Otto said. "Are you hearing this?"

"The readouts are still within the normal range," the engineer said. "You're probably fine."

"Probably?"

"You're fine."

He didn't sound sure.

When Otto was a little kid he'd often wake up at night with the paralyzing fear that a cat was under his bed—a big cat with bald patches and a milky eye. He could hear its claws, as long as knives, rustling the carpet. When he eventually worked up the courage to call out to his parents, it was usually Dad who came in. Dad, with his soothing songs and his reassurances

15:05 and his rough hands that gently stroked Otto's hair.

But sometimes his mother came in instead. She wouldn't even sit down on the bed.

One breath, she would tell him. *That's all it takes to calm down, if you really pay attention to it.*

Now Otto inhaled slowly, listening to the sound, trying to feel the air in his lungs and trying not to imagine the walls slamming inward and squashing him like a cherry tomato.

It worked, sort of.

14:30 *Thump*! Something else hit the vessel. Not a shark this time. The ground.

He peered through the glass, but it was still pitch black.

"I'm at the bottom," he said.

"Great," the engineer said. "Any signs of life?"

"I can't see anything."

"Are your lights on?"

14:00 Otto scanned the control panel, feeling foolish. He didn't remember anyone telling him how to turn the lights on.

There—a button marked *LIGHTS*. He pushed it.

Immediately the twin lamps clicked on, as bright as the sun.

13:35 Otto screamed.

Something was stuck to the dome. A tangle of

tentacles around a slimy purple mouth, sucking on the outside of the glass.

"What's going on out there?" the engineer demanded.

"Nothing. I mean, an octopus scared me. It was stuck to the dome."

Mom's voice: "You're deeper than any known species of octopus can go. Can you grab it?"

"I'll try." Otto grabbed the joysticks. He heard the mechanical arms rotate in their sockets, but he couldn't see them—the octopus was in the way.

Operating by feel, he pulled the joysticks backward and up, hoping to snag a tentacle. But the octopus reared back and launched itself away from the glass like a deflating balloon. A split second later it had vanished. Had it changed its skin color, released a cloud of ink, or simply disappeared into the shadows? It was too dark to tell.

"Sorry," Otto said. "I lost it." 12:30

Silence at the other end. Otto could feel his mother's disappointment.

"Understood," she said finally. "Keep looking."

Otto swallowed and leaned forward on both pedals. The tank treads rumbled and the submersible started to roll across the dark terrain.

Even with the lights, a cloud of black mist stopped

Otto from seeing far. Occasionally a big rock would loom in front of him and he'd have to swerve around it, but otherwise it was like driving across a feature-less wasteland at midnight. Flakes of sediment swirled around him like the shredded feathers of a raven.

"You're pretty close to your maximum depth," the engineer said. 'Watch out for holes in the ground. If you fall down one, you could implode.'

You could have mentioned that earlier, Otto thought. "How am I supposed to spot them? I can't see underneath me."

"I'm just saying, tread carefully. Watch the ground on the horizon."

"Horizon," Otto grumbled under his breath. "Can't see a thing."

A school of fish whipped past, scales shining in the halogen light, so fast that Otto barely registered they were there before they were gone. This was impossible. How was he supposed to grab anything that moved that fast?

Something emerged from the shadows up ahead. Too tall and narrow to be a rock. A stem of coral? No, too long, too perfectly curved.

Part of a sunken ship, perhaps. Otto turned in a slow circle. Yes, there was another stalk, the same as the first. And another. The submersible had rolled into a giant cage made of support-struts.

Or something. The stalks looked crumbly—not like `10:15`
metal, and not quite like wood.

"Do you guys know of any shipwrecks in this area?"
Otto asked.

Silence. `10:00`

"Hello?" Otto had the sudden sense that he'd
somehow traveled forward in time, and that he
was standing in the sunken ruins of what had once
been the *Endeavour*. Shivers rippled all over his
body.

"No," the engineer said finally. "There is nothing
on record. Why?"

Otto took a deep breath. "There's some strange
debris down here, that's all. It looks like a wreck."

He rolled closer to one of the struts. It was ghostly
white, with little divots in the surface where fish had
eaten it away.

It wasn't wood, or steel. It was bone. `09:30`

Otto's mouth fell open. He turned around in another
circle. He was in the center of a giant rib cage. A rotting
spine trailed away into the blackness.

"It's not a ship," he said. "It's a skeleton!"

"Otto," his mother said. "What kind of skeleton?" `09:05`

"A whale, I guess. A really, really big one." Then
something caught his eye just beyond the enormous

ribs. More bones—was that a gigantic *hand*?

He shivered. "Not a whale. This thing had arms."

"Can you break off a piece?" His mother sounded excited. "It may be too old to get anything useful from it, but it's worth a try."

"Part of one of the ribs?"

"Perfect. We have your coordinates—we'll send someone down to take pictures of the rest later."

Otto gripped the joysticks and maneuvred the robotic hands so they both gripped the nearest rib, one above the other. Then he twisted them in opposite directions.

08:20

Crack! The rib split and the top part broke off, clenched in Otto's mechanical fingers. He pushed the green button. The robotic arm swiveled out of sight. When it returned, the chunk of rib was gone. He wondered where the sample pouches were.

"OK," he said. "Got it."

"Great. Try to get something alive for the next one— or at least something with a little flesh on its bones."

08:00

Otto tilted forward on the pedals, rolling the submersible out of the rib cage. It was almost imposs- ible to imagine that something so big had once been alive. And it wasn't just the size. The pressure would kill most things, and the temperature was below zero down here—if not for the salt in the seawater it would have frozen solid.

Even harder to imagine was whatever had killed the beast. Otto could see scars on some of the bones, as if someone had taken an axe to them.

"Otto," the engineer said. "That storm is rolling in."

Unease clawed at Otto's heart. "What does that mean?"

"You're too deep to be affected and we're too big. So all it means is that we may lose radio contact."

"For how long? I—"

07:30

The submersible lurched downward. Otto yelled in panic. He hadn't been watching the ground closely enough. He was falling into a hole.

The pressure gauge shot upward. 114 MPa—the tested limit.

116 MPa.

119.

123.

07:20

Thinking quickly, Otto wrenched the joysticks apart. The robotic arms shot outward and slammed into the sides of the hole, stopping him from falling any farther.

The hull moaned ominously. It was under more pressure than it had been designed to take.

"What's going on down there?" the engineer demanded. His voice was fuzzy and faint.

07:00

"I've fallen down a hole," Otto said. "I've braced myself against the walls, but I can't climb out. If I let go with either hand, I'll fall. What should I do?"

The radio crackled. Otto could hear the engineer saying something, but he couldn't tell what.

"I didn't catch that," he said. "Can you say again?"

More crackling, but no trace of a voice.

Otto cursed. He was on his own.

There was a way out—he could dump the ballast and float back up to the surface. But if he did that, the mission was over, with only a solitary bone to show for it. He wouldn't be able to dive again until the storm passed.

But what choice did he have? He couldn't climb out, and he couldn't stay here. At any moment, the sub might implode.

06:30   Something moved above him.

He looked up in time to see a mass migration of fish. Squids darted past the top of the hole. Giant crabs scuttled over the top of it. Hulking sharks cruised by. Despite his mother's lessons, Otto didn't recognize any of these species. They must have evolved differently to cope with the pressure.

All these creatures were moving in the same direction. It would have been the perfect opportunity to catch something and complete his mission if he weren't stuck in this hole.

The hull creaked under the strain of all the `06:00` water. Otto's fingers hovered over the ballast-release switches. If he abandoned his mission, the flyrus might kill thousands of people. But if he didn't, he would be crushed to death. What could he do?

A huge black shadow swept across the top of the hole and then vanished.

Otto looked up, eyes wide. What was that? `05:30`

Perhaps it had been what all the other fish were fleeing from. It was certainly big enough.

"Can anyone hear me?" he said.

Not even a crackle from the radio.

"There's something alive down here," he continued. "Something huge. I think—"

He screamed as a dark shape rushed down into the hole. Huge tentacles closed around the dome.

No, not tentacles. Claws. The sub was clenched in a giant hand!

The robotic arms scraped the sides of the tunnel as something pulled the sub out of the hole. The sub's underwater weight was three tons. Whatever this thing was, it had unbelievable strength.

"Something's got me!" Otto shouted. "Help!" `05:00`

Suddenly he was face to face with the monster. It was like a crocodile that had grown to the size of a 747. Bulging muscles uncoiled beneath a shell of black scales. Yellow eyes as big as soccer balls peered through the glass at Otto.

The monster was so big that he couldn't even see all of it. Just the head, the hand, and something swirling in the distance that might have been a tail.

Otto sat perfectly still. Maybe if he didn't move the beast would decide he wasn't edible.

04:40 A gigantic mouth opened wide, revealing teeth like elephant tusks.

"Help!" Otto screamed again, but then the mouth clamped down. Teeth rammed the sub from all angles. One of the halogen lights cracked and went out.

An alarm wailed behind Otto's ears. The controls lit up with warning lights. One of them read: HULL INTEGRITY COMPROMISED. The creaking of the sub became a roar, like a rocket taking off.

04:00 The monster retreated, looking puzzled. It had probably never bitten anything that hadn't immediately turned to mush. It craned its head sideways for another attempt.

In desperation, Otto flicked every switch he could see. The sub lurched upward as the ballast disconnected from the base—

03:50 But the sea monster grabbed it before it was too far out of reach. Otto screamed as that enormous mouth filled his vision again. The creature had opened wider this time. He could see the spongy protrusions at the back of its throat. Its tongue looked like a moldy surfboard.

When the jaws closed around him this time the teeth didn't touch the sub. The monster was trying to swallow him whole!

03:30

The membranes at the back of the throat peeled back, ready to suck him into the purple pit.

Otto leaped into action. He stuck his robotic arms outward, jamming one into the roof of the creature's mouth and stabbing the other into its tongue.

Then he hit the green button.

The monster thrashed as the sub tried to rip out its tongue and put it in a sample pouch. Otto was flung forward and back inside the sub. It was like being crammed into a barrel and rolled down a hill.

02:50

But the thing still didn't open its jaws and spit out the sub. It was time for more drastic measures.

Otto tilted both feet as far forward as they would go.

Beneath him the treads spun at full speed. The sub couldn't move, so the treads churned up the beast's gums instead. Scraps of flesh floated up past the glass.

"Let me out!" Otto roared. He leaned back on the pedals, spinning the treads in the opposite direction, attacking the creature's gums anew.

A black cloud of blood filled the monster's mouth.

The throat opened, as if to swallow him—

And then a tide of vomit surged up the creature's throat. Otto screamed as the vile gunk swept up the sub and carried it out into the open ocean.

02:00 When the visibility cleared, he saw that the giant beast was being attacked. Drawn in by the blood, leech-like creatures swarmed all over its scales. Strange sharks with four eyes each latched onto its underbelly. A cloud of things that looked a bit like big seahorses with stinging tails appeared. Otto watched with fascination and horror as they burrowed under the monster's eyelid.

Seconds later the giant creature shuddered and went limp.

01:30 Freed of both the monster and the ballast, the sub was already starting to rise. Otto grabbed the joysticks, flung his mechanical arms downward and just managed to grab onto the dead leviathan.

The monster was heavy, but the sub was extremely buoyant without the ballast. It zoomed upward through the ocean with the giant creature trailing behind it, hundreds of parasites still attached.

The water got brighter and brighter. Soon he could see the surface, a shimmering curtain, and through it, the afternoon sun.

00:59 *Snap!* The hull cracked. A jet of saltwater hosed down the inside of the cockpit. Otto turned his face away from the freezing spray.

Just a few more seconds, he thought.

He could feel another leak springing by his feet. Soon his shoes were drenched. But he was almost there. Almost—

`00:50`

Splash! The sub burst through the surface into the afternoon sunlight. Otto stabbed frantically at the control panel until he found the control that released the seal around the glass dome. It rose up with a hiss and his ears popped as the pressure equalized.

The ship was right nearby. He could see his mother standing on the deck, staring at him.

"Hey!" he shouted, waving. "Is this enough weird life forms for you?"

She stared at the gigantic floating corpse, swarming with never-before-seen parasites from the mysterious depths of the ocean. A wild grin spread across her face. Otto had never seen her look so amazed.

She cleared her throat. "Well," she said. "It's a good start."

`00:00`

NUCLEAR FAMILY

30:00 "Stay right where you are," Mom said. "This place is dangerous."

"You said the contamination would be gone," Milla objected.

"I said it *should* be gone. But we need to be sure."

Milla looked around. The lake didn't look that bad. There were no plastic wrappers waltzing in the breeze, no mountains of discarded batteries, slicks of oil, or any of the other things she'd seen on her travels with her parents. Just a dusty slope leading down to a flat, green lake. A line of birch trees stood on the other side under a gray sky. It was oddly peaceful.

29:30 But thanks to the visor of the hazmat suit, she felt like she was seeing it all on television. They had been in Russia for two days, but she didn't feel like she had *experienced* it. The airport had been just like any other airport. The hotel in Moscow had been like any other hotel. Now here they were in the wilds of Siberia, and she couldn't smell it or touch it because of the hazmat suit.

She had begged to come on this trip. She had argued that it couldn't be more dangerous than staying home, where a deadly virus was sweeping the country. She hadn't realized she would be seeing Russia exclusively from behind glass.

`28:50`

"Don't get too close to the water," Dad said, his voice crackling through the suit's speakers.

Milla sighed. "I'm not moving."

Dad shuffled through the dirt toward the lake, waving a plastic cylinder in the air. An eerie clicking sound rang out from a speaker on his belt.

"Better hustle," Mom said. "These hazmat suits only have thirty minutes of air."

`28:20`

"I know, I know."

"What happened here again?" Milla asked.

"The Soviets built a reactor near here in 1945," Mom explained. "They spent ten years making nuclear weapons and dumping all the radioactive waste into this lake."

"That was a *long* time ago."

`28:00`

"Yes, but radiation fades really, really slowly. As recently as 1990, just standing on the shore of this lake for an hour would kill you."

Milla felt a little ill. "We'll be OK though, right? With the hazmat suits?"

"The suits will stop us from breathing any

radioactive particles, but the lead lining is pretty thin. Strong enough radiation could still penetrate it—that's why you shouldn't go too close to the lake."

"Stop it," Dad said. "You're scaring her."

He was right, but Milla didn't want to admit it.

"Why don't they make the suits thicker?"

"Lead is heavy. If the lining were thicker, you wouldn't be able to walk."

27:00 Milla already found it hard to walk. The suit felt heavy, like a medieval suit of armor. She noticed for the first time that nothing was growing in the dirt around the lake. No grass, no weeds, no wriggling earthworms.

She smiled weakly. "So I suppose a swim is out of the question."

Mom laughed. "Right. But if it's any consolation, the water is less than two feet deep."

Milla squinted at the lake. "Really?"

"Yep. After a disaster in 1968—"

"Polly," Dad warned.

"The Russians filled the lake with concrete blocks," Mom continued, "to stop the contaminants at the bottom from moving around."

26:30 "What kind of disaster?" Milla asked.

Dad shot Mom a pointed look.

"The lake dried up," Mom said. "The wind blew the

sediment from the bottom across the nearest town."

"Oh no! Did anyone get sick?"

"That was a long time ago, sweetie—" Dad began.

"Half a million people got radiation poisoning," Mom said. She didn't sound excited anymore, but at least she was telling the truth.

Milla stared into the green, still water. "That's why the UN sent us here," she said.

-26:00-

"Right. We can verify that no radiation remains and that the concrete is doing its job. To make sure it never happens again." Mom turned to Dad, who was waving the Geiger counter in the air near the water. "How are we doing, Trent?"

"It's not good," Dad said. "Give me a minute."

-25:45-

Milla stared up at a small airplane that had just appeared over the distant mountains. She had traveled with Mom and Dad to many toxic places, ranging from sun-blasted desert dumping grounds to a floating garbage patch in the middle of the ocean, but she'd never been anywhere radioactive.

"What does radiation do to a person?" she asked.

-25:00-

"Depends on how much you're exposed to," Mom said. "If it's only a little bit, nothing. If it's a bit more, it can interfere with your DNA. You might get cancer later in life or have children with birth defects."

"And if it's a lot?"

41

"It's like getting burned," Mom said. "Your skin peels off. You start vomiting, your brain gets—"

"That's enough," Dad said.

Milla appreciated that Dad wanted to protect her, but not knowing was even scarier. Maybe she shouldn't have insisted on joining this expedition.

"It's not going to happen to us, sweetie," Mom said. "The hazmat suits will protect us."

24:20 Dad's shoulders slumped. "Correct—but we'd be dead without them, according to these readings." He pocketed the Geiger counter. "The levels haven't died down as much as we would have hoped. We're going to have to check the river as well. It's possible that radioactive particles are seeping into the Arctic Ocean."

"Come on," Mom said. "Let's get back to the truck."

24:00 The truck was parked nearby, but it would take them a long time to get in. They would have to enter the airlock, get sprayed by high-pressure hoses, drain the airlock, and take off their hazmat suits before they could move on.

Milla took one last look up at the Russian sky.

"That plane's awfully close," she said.

Mom and Dad looked up.

There was a moment of silence as they contemplated the sight—a small airplane, tilted forward and banking slightly, thin loops of smoke unspooling from one engine as it zoomed closer and closer to the ground.

It was headed straight for them.

"Run!" Mom screamed.

`23:45`

Milla was the slowest to react. She had spent so long convincing herself that they were safe. But when Mom and Dad turned to flee toward the truck, she did too, the unease in her chest exploding into full-blown panic.

She ran as quickly as she could, but in the lead-lined hazmat suit, that wasn't very fast. The roaring of the plane engines got louder and louder, filling her helmet and hurting her ears. Her feet sank too far into the dust with every step. It was like one of those nightmares in which a monster was chasing her through quicksand.

She was falling behind. Her parents wouldn't leave her—they must think she was with them.

"Mom!" she screamed, so loud her throat bled. "Dad! Wait!"

But she couldn't even hear her own voice over the screaming of the plane. There was no way they would hear her.

`23:00`

Dad had almost reached the truck when—

Smash! The plane hit the lake behind them with a sound like a shopping cart crashing into a drum kit. The sky went black. A hailstorm of concrete whipped past Milla, punching holes in the dust all around her and thunking against her helmet. As she fell, a propeller shot past, missing her by inches. She landed facedown in the dirt.

Then the lake itself fell out of the sky in a thunderous downpour. Milla was crushed beneath the deluge of radioactive water.

22:45 She might have blacked out for a few seconds. It was hard to tell. But at some point she found herself lying in the mud, ears ringing, limbs aching.

"Milla!" The voice had been shouting for a while, but she hadn't recognized her own name until now. Someone was shaking her shoulder.

"Mom?" she groaned, rolling over. All her muscles ached.

22:30 Her mother's hazmat suit was spattered with so much mud and concrete dust that she looked like an orc or a troll.

"Milla," she said. "Are you hurt?"

"I . . . no. I don't think so. Are you OK?"

"Polly! Milla!" Dad's voice.

Milla turned her head but couldn't see him. Just the twisted ruins of the plane, half-submerged in the lake. The cockpit was empty—either no one had been in it or the pilot had been thrown clear on impact.

"We're over here," Mom called. She didn't raise her hand.

"Are you hurt?" Milla asked again.

21:00

"I think my arm is broken," Mom muttered. "I'll check it when we're in the truck. Do you still have suit pressure?"

Milla suddenly realized how much danger they were in. She and Mom were covered in radioactive slime. If either of them had the smallest puncture in their suits . . .

Milla pinched the fabric around her wrist. Her fingers left dents, but they smoothed themselves out. Her suit still had pressure.

"I'm OK," she said. "You?"

"I can't check. My arm . . ."

Milla pinched Mom's suit. It still seemed to be pressurized.

Dad stumbled into view. He was almost as dirty as they were. "Is everyone all right?" he demanded.

"You tell us," Mom said. "How much radiation are we being exposed to right now?"

"We'll be OK," Dad said. "So long as we get into the airlock and get these suits cleaned up right away."

"Uh, Dad?" Milla pointed to the truck.

20:00

Mom and Dad gasped. The airplane propeller had impaled the truck, shearing through the metal and glass. The insides were open to the air, splattered with radioactive slop.

"We'll have to go to the nearest town," Mom said.

"It's more than five miles away," Dad said.

"How long until we run out of oxygen?" Milla asked.

"We have plenty of oxygen. But every time we exhale, that increases the amount of carbon dioxide—CO_2—in the suit. Once four per cent of the air is CO_2, we can't breathe the air." Dad always gave too much information when he was nervous. "In about twenty minutes, the CO_2 will reach toxic levels."

19:25 They stared at one another for a moment. Milla did the math in her head. Could they really run at eighteen miles per hour—almost as fast as an Olympic sprinter—in lead-lined hazmat suits?

"We have to try," Mom said.

Dad shook his head. "We should call for help. I've got my mobile in my pocket."

"*Inside* your hazmat suit," Mom said. "Right?"

18:30 Dad said nothing.

"So we can't get to it," Mom continued. "It's useless."

It took Milla a moment to work out what Dad was thinking. He could take off his suit and phone for help. He would be exposed to a massive dose of radiation. But she and Mom would survive.

"No," Mom said. "We run until there's no more air, then we take our helmets off."

"And get cancer?"

"There's no other way."

"I could—"

"The river," Milla said.

Mom and Dad looked at her.

"You said there's a river near here," Milla said. "Is it closer than the village?"

"About half a mile away," Dad said.

"We could wash our suits in the river and then take them off. I know we don't want to contaminate the water—"

"But it's better than getting killed," Mom said. "Good thinking, Milla. Let's go."

They scrambled to their feet and started to run around the lake toward the row of birch trees.

"What about the pilot?" Milla asked.

"If there was one—and it didn't fly like a plane with a pilot—then there's no point looking for him," Mom said. "A crash like that, into radioactive concrete . . . there's just no way he could have survived. I'm sorry, honey."

Surely someone should try to recover his body? Milla thought. But probably not them, and not now. She saved her breath for running.

The forest was just ahead—a labyrinth of towering birches with straight gray trunks and scabby branches. Milla followed her parents in.

17:50

16:20

16:00

47

14:50

It was uphill, which was hard work in the lead-lined suit. There was no trail. They had to push through a mess of bracken and fallen branches. The leaves above blotted out most of the daylight. Milla kept having to look up and around to make sure she hadn't lost her parents.

"So we're getting radiationed right now?" she said. "Even through the suits?"

"Irradiated," Dad corrected. "And yes, but not much."

"How much?"

"I think over the next twenty minutes we'll absorb about as much radiation as you'd get during five or six medical X-rays."

"Oh," Milla said. "That doesn't sound *too* bad."

"No. It's not great, but we're not likely to have any long-term effects, provided we get the suits cleaned before our helmets come off. The river—"

"Stop," Mom said.

13:30

Milla froze. "What is it?"

Mom was staring at a gap between two distant trees. "Did you see that?"

"See what?"

"We don't have time for this," Dad said.

"Something moved," Mom said. "Up ahead."

"Probably just a bird. We have to keep moving."

"It was way bigger than a bird."

"A feral cat, then," Dad said. "Come on."

"Bigger than a cat."

"Well, what was it?"

Mom didn't answer.

"We're running out of air," Dad said.

Mom took one last look at the shadows between the trees. "OK," she said. "But try not to make too much noise."

They kept walking. It was hard to be quiet in such heavy suits. Milla winced as each twig crunched underfoot, knowing the sounds were muffled by the helmet and must be much louder outside.

Soon they reached the top of the hill. Milla could see the river sparkling in the distance. They had about ten minutes left to reach it.

She heard her father let out a moan.

"What's wrong?" she asked.

Dad looked confused. "That wasn't me," he said.

They both looked at Milla's mother. She shook her head, eyes wide.

The sound echoed out again. It sounded like a man crying in the distance. A mournful wail, dying away into the silence.

Goosebumps erupted all over Milla's body. Who else was in this forest with them? And why didn't they

12:00

09:50

09:00

sound quite human?

"Keep moving," Mom whispered.

They shuffled down the hill, watching their surroundings. Milla listened carefully but couldn't hear anything over her own breaths and pumping heart.

08:30 "Almost there." Dad's voice was low and even. "We won't be able to swim in the river. The suits are too heavy. So we'll have to crawl across to the far side. Make sure your head is completely submerged. Got it?"

Milla was about to reply when a monster leapt out of the shrubs in front of them.

It was a wolf.

07:50 Milla had never seen a wolf in real life before. It was bigger than the biggest dog she'd ever met, with enormous, dirty paws and long, saliva-slicked fangs. The matted fur around its jaws was encrusted with old blood. A cloudy, moon-like eye stared at them from a pink-rimmed socket.

Milla only saw it for a fraction of a second. It blasted by, close enough to knock her off her feet, and vanished into the trees on the other side of the clearing. Its footfalls faded away like the hoof beats of a galloping horse.

Dad dragged Milla to her feet. "Are you OK?"

06:30 She nodded, heart pounding. "Where did it go?"

"It's toying with us."

"What do we do?" Mom asked.

"We could climb a tree," Milla said. Then she remembered Mom's broken arm.

"We head for the river," Dad said. "We don't really have a choice."

`06:00`

Another wail on the wind.

This must be what a wolf howl sounds like in real life, Milla thought.

"It sounds like there's more than one of them," she said.

"The first one may be trying to herd us toward the rest of the pack. Come on."

`05:30`

They sprinted down the hill to the river. There was no point being slow and careful anymore. The wolf knew where they were—their only hope was to get to the water before it came back.

But couldn't wolves swim? Dogs certainly could.

The water sparkled between the trees. They were almost at the edge of the forest.

Too late.

`05:00`

Two wolves exploded out of the forest in front of them. Their huge ears stood straight up like sails and ropes of drool hung from their slavering mouths. They stared intensely at the three humans with their strange, milky eyes.

"Run!" Dad screamed.

"No!" Milla grabbed his arm. "Don't move."

One of the wolves growled—a sound like an idling motor.

Radiation can cause birth defects.

"Milla," Mom hissed.

"They're blind," Milla whispered. "See?"

They stood in silence for a moment, looking at the wolves' clouded eyes.

"And they can't smell us through the hazmat suits," Milla whispered. "Look at their ears. They're going purely on sound."

A bird chittered nearby. One of the wolves turned its head toward the sound, but neither one took a step. It hadn't been toying with them earlier, Milla realized. It had just taken a guess at where they were and charged.

04:00

The growling wolf sniffed the wind. It kicked its back legs as if wiping mud off its paws. The other wolf huffed angrily.

Then both wolves started moving slowly toward the humans.

"Back away," Dad whispered.

03:20

"They'll hear us!" Mom replied.

Milla ignored both of them. She leaned down and picked up a lump of rock about the size of a tennis ball.

One of the wolves barked. The sound was as loud as a trombone at full blast. It must have heard her move.

Milla hurled the rock as far as she could. It flew silently through the air and smashed down into the foliage in the distance.

03:00

Both wolves spun toward the sound. With a swing of their dirty tails, they bounded away into the undergrowth.

"Go!" Milla hissed. "Quick!"

They dashed down the hill and burst out of the forest into the light. Milla's boots sank into the mud by the river's edge. The closer she got to the rushing water, the safer she felt. The wolves wouldn't hear them over the hissing and gurgling of the river.

02:30

She threw herself into the water. As Dad had predicted, she sank to the bottom immediately, weighed down by her suit. She crawled forward until she was in the deepest part of the river, lying on her back and staring into the rippling sun. The radioactive mud swirled out of the creases in her suit and drifted away like smoke.

We made it, she thought. *We actually made it!*

And then a message flashed on her visor.

WARNING: CO$_2$ AT TOXIC LEVELS.

01:55

She had run out of air. And she was at the bottom of a river.

She looked around. Mom and Dad must have finished scrubbing themselves and resurfaced. They were nowhere to be seen. She opened her mouth to shout for help, but the air inside her suit was now toxic. If she breathed in so she could call out, she might die.

She tried to swim up to the surface, but it was impossible. The suit was too heavy and the current too strong. She could barely stand, let alone swim.

`01:35` Her lungs burned. She was getting dizzy.

She was going to have to take off the suit.

Milla tore open the rubber seals over her shoulders. Freezing water rushed into her hazmat suit, stinging her skin. It was all she could do not to gasp. She popped the safety clamps around her helmet and pulled it off.

The full force of the river hit her, pummeling her face. The hazmat suit was tangled around her ankles. She kicked it off and swam toward the surface. At least she *thought* it was the surface. She was getting dizzy and the river was bouncing her around like a popcorn kernel.

`01:05` The world was starting to get dark. She was going to black out.

Just one more minute! she begged.

Swirling, pounding, rushing and—

`00:59` *Splash!* Her head exploded into the daylight. She took a gasp of crisp, bracing air and felt the oxygen course through her body, bringing new life to her aching muscles.

Mom and Dad were waving from the riverbank. Milla waved back as she let herself float toward the shore. She took in the sun, the clouds, the trees, the water, and sucked in another deep breath. `00:10`

That, she thought, *is the smell of the Siberian wilderness.* `00:00`

CARNAGE

30:00 "**P**olice, fire, or ambulance?"

"Police," Kim said.

"Are you in a safe location?"

Kim looked around at the bustling intersection. It looked so normal that he almost couldn't believe what he had just seen. "Uh, yes," he said, trying to sound as adult as possible. "I think so."

"Where are you calling from?"

"I'm at . . ." Kim looked around for a street sign. A traffic light turned red. Pedestrians started moving past him. Someone bumped into his shoulder and walked away without apology.

29:40 "Corner of London Circuit and Ainslie Place," he said. "In Civic."

"What is your emergency?" The man spoke like someone who took hundreds of these calls every day and knew that most of them were nothing.

"I just saw two guys walk out of a bank," Kim said, "and I think one of them had a gun under his arm."

"Can you describe the men?"

Kim tried to think back. But although it had only just happened, he couldn't recall the two men at all.

"I think one of them was tall? Maybe?"

`29:20`

The phone operator sighed. "Can you describe what they were wearing?"

"The one with the gun had a knee-length coat. Black, or maybe brown."

"Was that the tall one, or the other one?"

Kim cringed. "I'm not sure. Sorry, I was looking at the gun."

"What kind of gun was it?"

Kim didn't know much about guns, but he had seen them on TV. "A shotgun, I think."

"Where did the two men go?" The operator sounded marginally more interested now.

"Around the corner onto Riverside Lane."

"Police are on their way. Please stay on the line."

"How long will they take?"

`28:35`

"A car was dispatched as soon as you told us your location. They're now about six minutes away."

Kim looked around at the crowded street. Everyone was moving in a different direction. He tried to imagine the cops showing up and asking people, "Did you see two men about six minutes ago, one of whom may have been tall and wearing a brown or black coat?"

But the two men weren't gone yet. They had disappeared around the corner only a minute ago. Kim was sure he could find them again.

What would the superheroes on TV do? he asked himself.

"I'll follow them," he said. "To get a better description."

"I strongly advise you not to do that," the operator said.

In books and movies the heroes always acted immediately. They didn't stop to worry about consequences—they just ran into the burning building or jumped overboard to save the drowning swimmer, or whatever.

27:30 But Kim was a thinker. He often worried that someday he would get the chance to be a hero, and he would hesitate too long. What if this was his chance right now?

He stared at the alley where the two men had disappeared. *What would a superhero do?* he asked himself again.

27:00 He ran to the corner of Riverside Lane and peered in. It was a narrow alley, deserted except for three women at the other end. One of them pushed a stroller. He couldn't see the two men.

Kim was unsure whether to feel disappointed or

relieved. They must have reached the other end and turned either right or left. Kim decided to run up there and have a look around.

He made it about ten steps.

As he passed a doorway a hand reached out of the shadows and grabbed him by the collar. The cold muzzle of the shotgun pressed against his temple.

"See?" a voice said. "I told you he saw the gun."

Kim's heart skipped a beat. He wondered if it was possible for a kid to have a heart attack. He still had the phone in his hand, but before he could shout for help one of the men snatched it from him and ended the call.

The guy with the gun was a lanky man with sallow skin and stringy blond hair. His coat was dark blue, not brown or black. He stared at Kim with enormous eyes that never seemed to blink.

26:10

The other man was built like a gorilla. Big shoulders, short legs, and a high-domed head that hung forward, as though he'd spent his formative years hunched over a laptop. Stubbly lumps encrusted his square jaw like barnacles on the *Titanic*. He was holding a briefcase— another thing Kim had pretty much only seen on TV.

Neither of them were especially tall.

25:40

"How much did you tell the cops?" the gunman said.

Kim talked rapidly. "I said I saw two men coming

out of a bank. A skinny guy with blond hair, a dark blue coat and a shotgun, and a bulky man with stubble and a briefcase."

He had hoped that the two men would flee when they heard this. They didn't.

"What do you want to do with him?" the gorilla asked.

"Can't let him go," the lanky guy said. "He's a witness."

"This is some kind of joke, right?" Kim said. "That's just a fake gun, and there are hidden cameras watching my reaction?"

He didn't really believe it. But if the two thugs thought he did, they might let him go.

No luck. "Listen up, kid," the gunman said. He had a voice like a blues singer with the flu. "We're going to take a walk. I'm going to be right behind you. If you try to run, I'll shoot you. If you talk to anyone, I'll shoot you *and* them and whoever else happens to be nearby for good measure."

The gorilla smiled, showing chipped teeth. "He's not a great shot," he said, "but with a gun like that, you don't have to be."

"Do as we say," the gunman continued, "and you'll live a long, happy life with a great story to tell at parties. Got that?"

Kim doubted it, but he nodded.

"Smart boy," the gunman said. "Let's go."

He slipped the shotgun back into his coat and pushed Kim out of the doorway so suddenly he fell over. The damp asphalt scraped his palms and bruised his tailbone.

23:20

"Get up," the gorilla growled. He didn't need a gun of his own to sound threatening.

Kim scrambled to his feet.

"Walk that way." The gorilla pointed back the way they had come, toward the bank.

Kim shuffled back up the alley. He couldn't hear any footsteps. Perhaps the two thugs had fled in the opposite direction.

He looked back over his shoulder. No such luck. The two men loomed right behind him. The gun wasn't pointed at him, but he could feel it waiting beneath the blue coat.

"Eyes straight ahead," the gunman hissed.

23:00

Kim turned back to face the road. When they reached the mouth of the alley, the main street was as busy as before. Pedestrians strode back and forth, oblivious to the hostage situation playing out right in front of them.

"Left," the gorilla said.

Kim turned. They walked past shops, bus stops, and

road signs toward an underground parking garage.

Before they reached it, a police car pulled up to the curb. Two police officers, one female, one male, stepped out of the car and started walking toward Kim and the thugs.

22:00 "Don't do anything stupid," the gunman said, just loud enough for Kim to hear.

Kim kept walking toward the cops who were approaching them.

He glanced at their faces as they were about to pass by. If one had shot him a questioning gaze, or stared pointedly at the men behind him, he might have tried to warn them. But neither of them even looked at him. They were searching for two men, one tall, one with a brown or black coat. Not two men and a child, all of average height, one with a blue coat.

The police passed by without incident and disappeared into the crowd behind them.

"Good boy," the gunman said after a pause. "Left again."

Wondering if he had just signed his own death warrant, Kim obeyed and turned left into the underground parking garage.

20:45 "Wait," the gorilla said. He jogged back out onto the street. A curved mirror hung high on the wall, designed to show drivers hazards around the corner.

Kim watched the gorilla's reflection crouch next to the police car for a second. Then he turned and walked back to the car park.

20:05

"Good thinking," the gunman said. "How many tires?"

"One's enough."

Kim felt a sinking feeling in his chest. The police wouldn't be able to follow with slashed tires. And if the gorilla had a knife, that was bad news.

The underground car park was cavernous and nearly deserted. A white van stood alone in the shadows between the fluorescent overhead lights. *The perfect vehicle for two killers*, Kim thought.

18:55

But no. They walked past the van to a gray sedan hidden behind it. The gunman opened the passenger-side door, which was unlocked. Kim had the sudden feeling that they didn't have the key. The car was probably stolen.

The gunman pulled a roll of duct tape off the seat and tossed it to the gorilla. Then he pulled the gun out of his coat and took aim at Kim.

"Hold your hands behind your back," he said.

Kim did.

18:20

The gorilla wound the tape around his wrists, so tight that Kim's hands swelled up. Then he crouched and bound Kim's ankles too.

The gorilla opened the trunk, tossed in the brief-case, and gestured to Kim. "Get in."

Kim peered into the cramped darkness of the trunk. "Are you serious?"

The gorilla grabbed him by the hair with a mighty fist. Kim yelped as follicles were torn out of his scalp.

"Get in," the gorilla repeated.

Unable to use his hands or feet, Kim sat on the edge of the trunk and rolled in. The gorilla didn't let go of his hair until he was inside. The thin carpet offered no protection from the hubcap of the spare tire beneath. Everything smelled like oil and old, dry mud.

17:00 — The gorilla peeled one last length of tape off the roll and plastered it over Kim's mouth. Panicked breaths whistled through his nostrils.

With a tremendous *whooshing* sound, the gorilla slammed the lid shut. Kim found himself sealed in the blackness, claustrophobia rushing in.

16:40 — He had been warned never to get into the trunk of a car, not even as a joke. His parents had told him he could suffocate or die of heatstroke, and if the car was in motion, a sharp turn or sudden stop could throw him against the walls.

The car rocked as the doors closed. The engine coughed and rumbled. Kim rolled sideways as the car lurched forward.

What could he use? He fumbled around in the **16:00** dark. He could feel a magazine, or perhaps a street directory. There was also scrunched up paper, probably from a burger. Not helpful.

The only other thing was the briefcase.

The clasps were the same as those on his trumpet case. It was tricky to unlatch them with his hands behind his back, but Kim managed it. The case popped open, and he rummaged around inside.

Papers. More papers. A leather-bound book, perhaps a diary.

Kim gasped as his hand closed around something sharp. Not like a knife—more like a piece of broken glass. But he didn't think it had broken the skin. **14:50**

He gripped the object by the blunt end, which was hard and lumpy, and started hacking away at the tape around his wrists. The first stab didn't pierce the tape. The second missed it altogether and pricked the inside of his wrist. He suppressed a squeak, took aim a third time and pushed the sharp edge through the tape. It started to tear. **14:20**

He could hear the gunman's muffled voice over the engine. "Yes, sir, we got it. They opened the safe deposit box pretty quick once they saw the fake gun."

Fake gun? Kim felt so stupid. But that didn't mean he was safe—the gorilla had a knife.

"We got to the tellers before they could trigger the silent alarm," the gunman continued. "The staff and customers are tied up and the doors are locked. But there was a witness outside the bank. A Middle Eastern-looking kid, blue shirt, gray shoes. We have him in the trunk."

14:00

A pause.

"Are you sure? That seems harsh."

Kim's heart beat faster.

"Yes, sir. Understood."

"What did he say?" the gorilla asked.

"He—wait. Where's the package?"

"In the trunk."

The car stopped.

"You left it with him?"

"He's not going anywhere."

Kim held the briefcase shut with his elbow as he tried to lock it behind his back.

The car door opened. "What were you thinking?" the gunman demanded.

Kim didn't hear the gorilla's response. He kept fumbling with the clasps.

He just got them closed in time. The gunman opened the trunk. Kim squinted against the light.

13:00

The briefcase was closed, but he hadn't had time to put the sharp object back inside. It was tucked under him.

Don't look in the case, he thought. *Don't look in* 12:55
the case.

A wailing siren echoed on the breeze. The gunman didn't say anything. Nor did he open the case. He simply slammed the trunk shut again. Kim heard his footsteps crunch around to the door again. It closed, and the car started moving.

"Cops are coming," the gunman said. "We have to get out of here." 12:00

Kim kept digging at the tape holding his wrists together. Soon he'd punched enough holes in it that he could tear through the plastic like perforated paper.

As soon as his wrists were separated he realized how much his shoulders hurt. He flexed his sore arms and got to work on the tape binding his ankles. He left the other strip over his mouth. It was unpleasant, but if the two thugs opened the trunk unexpect- edly, he wanted to be able to pretend that he was still trussed up. 11:40

Soon Kim's legs were free—but *he* wasn't. He was still trapped in the trunk of a car, and it sounded like it was going quite fast. The wheels were thrumming against smooth blacktop and the engine growled at an even pace.

Where were they taking him? And what would they do with him once they arrived? The gunman's voiced echoed through his head: *Are you sure? That seems harsh.*

11:00 Now that his hands were more mobile, Kim searched the trunk again. He had heard there was some kind of legal requirement that all modern cars had an open button inside the trunk in case someone became trapped. If he found it, he could jump out and run as soon as the car stopped at an intersection.

But if the button was there, he couldn't find it in the pitch blackness. The carpet was smooth and featureless.

Maybe he could force the trunk open. He lay on his back, braced his feet against the inside of the lid and pushed with all his might.

There was a creaking sound, but that was it. The metal didn't move at all. He would be stuck in here until the two thugs opened the trunk. And the sharp object, whatever it was, wasn't much of a weapon.

10:20 The spare tire was digging into Kim's back. It gave him an idea. He peeled back the carpet—with great difficulty, since he was lying on top of it—and ran his hands over the spare tire. It was smooth around the sides and the tread was still ridged on the circumference. Never used. It was also thinner than a proper tire. It had probably been designed just to get the car to the nearest service station in the event of a blowout.

Kim lifted it up. As he was hoping, a tire iron lay **10:00** underneath.

There was no room to give it a practice swing, but it felt heavy enough to do some damage. The guy with the knife wouldn't get too close to him if he had this.

The car turned a corner and slowed down. Then it turned another corner, went up a slight incline, and rocked over several speed bumps. A while after that it stopped. **09:05**

The doors opened on both sides. Kim braced himself. This was it. He would escape or die trying.

He clenched his sweaty fist around the tire iron. If only it were like a video game, where he could make as many attempts as he wished. The two thugs were much bigger than he was, and they knew where they were. Did he stand a chance?

His chest hurt. He blinked quickly, trying to pre-emptively adjust his eyes to the brightness that would flood in when the trunk was opened. Hot air rushed into his nose with every breath.

What were they waiting for? Did they somehow know he was free? **08:30**

Kim's mind raced as he tried to work out how that would change things. They might unlock the trunk from a distance and then instruct him to get out. He wouldn't be close enough to use the tire iron. No, wait—they didn't have the keys. Or did they?

He listened for conversation. There was silence outside the vehicle. No voices, no traffic, no footsteps.

08:00 Feeling absurd, he thumped the floor twice as though knocking on a door. He had been hoping to provoke a reaction of some kind, but there was nothing.

The heat in the trunk was starting to become stifling. Suddenly it dawned on Kim that they didn't need to open the trunk to dispose of him. They could simply leave him locked in the trunk of a stolen car in the summer heat. In just a matter of hours he would be dead!

He ripped the tape off his mouth. His lips stung as the dry, cracked skin was pulled off. He ignored the pain. "Help!" he screamed. "Somebody help me!"

07:35 No response. The car might be parked in the middle of the desert for all he knew.

He braced his feet against the lid again. When he couldn't push it open, he tried kicking it. He pounded the lock until his feet were sore, then he tried slamming the tire iron into it. No luck. In fact, he feared he might have mangled the lock so badly that even someone with the key couldn't open the trunk.

He tried to steady his breathing. If the trunk was airtight, he might suffocate. He couldn't afford to use up too much oxygen too quickly.

Think, he told himself. *You can't open the trunk, but* `06:30`
you can't stay here. So what do you do?

He gasped. How could he have been so foolish? In
his mom's car, there was a hatch that connected the
trunk to the back seat. They had used it only recently
when they'd bought a new ladder. Perhaps this car had
something similar.

He shoved the backs of the seats, and immediately
felt a little give. A crack of light sliced through the
gloom. He pushed again, and the hatch popped open,
revealing a square tunnel into the rear passenger seat
of the car. The gap looked just wide enough. `05:50`

Kim squeezed his shoulders through. The light was
blinding after so long in the blackness of the trunk.
It was louder out here too. He could hear the distant
rumble of traffic, the blaring of a horn, the clatter of a
shopping cart.

At least he was close to a populated area. He thought
about shouting for help again, but for all he knew the
two thugs hadn't gone far.

He pulled his hips through the hole and tumbled
into the rear footwell. He sucked in a lungful of air—
not exactly fresh but better than it had been in the
trunk.

The horn blasted again. Closer now. `05:20`

Kim sat up so he could look out the window—

Then he immediately realized why the two thugs had parked here.

They had abandoned the car on the railroad tracks.

And a train was coming.

04:30 At the moment it was just a speck on the horizon. But the car was already humming as the tracks picked up the vibrations. The train's brakes were screaming, but Kim doubted that it would be able to stop in time.

He fumbled with the door. It wouldn't open. Panicking, he tried the other side. It was stuck too. Child-safe locks, Kim guessed.

He clambered into the front passenger seat and clawed at the door. This one popped open and he fell out onto the tracks. The coarse gravel in the rail bed crunched underneath him.

04:00 He rolled sideways and scrambled to his feet. The train was still a way off, but that wouldn't save him. The walls on either side of the tracks were sheer concrete, ten feet high and topped by chain-link fencing. Kim whirled around with growing dismay. The walls seemed to go on forever. There was no way out. He couldn't go back to the level crossing where the car had driven onto the tracks, because that would mean running toward the speeding train. He was going to have to flee in the opposite direction and hope that the train stopped before it hit him.

The horn blared again. The train would be here in a moment. He had to go, now.

But even if it didn't hit him, it was definitely going [03:30] to collide with the car. The force would turn it into a thousand pieces of debris, rocketing through the air with deadly force. How was Kim supposed to get far enough away to survive that?

He wondered if it was possible to drive the car farther up the tracks. But the engine had stopped. He had no idea how to start a car without a key.

The clatter of approaching wheels was deafening now. [03:00]

What would a superhero do?

No time to think it through. He just had to hope it would work. Kim ran over to the trunk and wrenched it open. The tire iron lay inside. He snatched it up and tried to close the trunk again, but he had damaged it too badly from inside. It kept popping open. So instead he ran around to the hood, stepped up onto it and ran onto the roof. It buckled slightly beneath his weight as the car rocked on its suspension. If he fell, he wouldn't have time for a second try. [02:30]

Kim hefted the tire iron, crouched, and jumped.

He flew through the air toward the concrete wall, arms outstretched. For a frightening second he thought he was going to fall back onto the tracks and be pulverized by the speeding train. But the height of the car and the length of the tire iron were just enough. The end of the iron hooked into the chain link fence and Kim found himself hanging almost five feet above the tracks.

02:20 He hauled himself up, face sweaty, shoulders screaming, and grabbed the fence with his other hand. Leaving the tire iron hanging from the mesh he clambered upward, deafened by the shrieking of the approaching train's brakes.

He was about to climb over the fence when he saw the two thugs running up the hill toward him.

He couldn't drop back down. The train was almost upon him. But he couldn't climb over—they would grab him. He hung there, paralyzed.

01:45 "How could you not check that it was still in the case?" the gorilla was shouting.

"The cops were coming!" the gunman yelled back. "*You're* the one who put it in there with him in the first place. Hey!" He spotted Kim clinging to the fence. "The bloodstone! Do you have it?"

"The what?" Kim demanded.

The gorilla drew his knife. "The bloodstone!" he roared. "Give it to me!"

"Drop the knife!" someone else bellowed.

Kim turned his head to see four police officers

charging up the other side of the hill, all wearing body armor. Two of them had tasers pointed at the gunman and the gorilla.

The two thugs groaned and dropped to their knees. The gunman lobbed the knife away.

`00:45`

Kim scrambled over the chain-link fence and collapsed onto the ground, safe at last. He was just in time. As he turned to look back down at the tracks, he saw the train rocket toward the sedan. The trunk was still open. He just had time to observe the object he had cut through the duct tape with—a ruby as big as a tennis ball—before the train smashed into the car. Wheels exploded outward, metal crumpled, glass turned to dust, and the ruby burst like a firecracker, dissolving into a thousand glittering chunks.

`00:00`

CHILLING

30:00 **"I**t's simple," Hope said. "You give them the form. You check that they haven't marked any of these highlighted boxes. Then you send them over to me, and I'll give them the injection."

Audrey looked at the stacks of syringes in the walk-in fridge. The fly virus—or "flyrus," as the newspapers had started calling it after "fly flu" failed to catch on—was almost always fatal. What if she missed something on the paperwork? Someone could die.

Her friends had earned work experience positions in bookshops and cafes. How had Audrey wound up in such a serious role? Yes, she did want to be a doctor someday, but this was too much too quickly.

"After I've done my bit," Hope continued, "give them an ice pack from the fridge and sit them down in one of those chairs. Note the time. We have to observe them for fifteen minutes before we let them go."

"What am I looking for?"

29:00 "If anyone goes pale or you notice a rash, let me know. Also if they complain of itching or nausea. By the way, you should wash your hands before we arrive."

Audrey turned to the sink. The Mobile Treatment Facility, or MTF, was no more than a powered shipping crate on the back of a semitrailer, but it was better equipped than some hospitals. In addition to the sink, it had a kettle, a microwave, a defibrillator, a file cabinet, a cupboard full of bandages, and an enormous walk-in fridge. A small, round window—the kind you might find in a submarine or a spaceship—revealed the gloomy city streets as they rolled past.

28:30

Today was day one of the immunization program. Right now hundreds of vehicles like this one were zooming toward infection hotspots all over the country. The goal was to get the whole population vaccinated within two weeks.

Audrey scrubbed her hands in the sink, dried them on a paper towel, and threw the towel into a medical waste bin. Then she sat down on the stool next to Hope.

28:00

"Should I be wearing a face mask?" she asked. "Since all these sick people will be coming in here?"

"The vaccine is designed to prevent the disease, not to cure it. Anyone who's already infected will go to the hospital, not here."

"What about people who don't know they're infected?"

"The infected start coughing up blood within thirty minutes of exposure," Hope said, "so that's unlikely. They also go pale, get sweaty, and show bruising around the eyes. And anyway, the disease isn't airborne. You don't need a face mask."

"How *does* it spread?"

"Through blood and saliva. Hence the hand washing, and—"

"Didn't you just say they *cough up blood*?" Audrey demanded. "What if I get some on me?"

"If you do, clean it off right away—but like I said, the people you're treating won't be sick. And you're already vaccinated, so even if you're exposed to the virus, you won't get it." Hope looked around, making sure everything was in order. "It says this on the form, but don't put through anyone over seventy or anyone under two for vaccination."

"Why not?"

"It's a live vaccine. Each syringe contains a modified version of the flyrus."

"We're giving people the virus to stop them from getting the virus?"

Hope looked like she had explained this many, many times before. "It's a weaker strain, so it will teach the patient's immune system to fight off the real thing. But very young and very old people don't have

78

strong immune systems, so we can only protect them by vaccinating everybody else."

The MTF shuddered to a halt.

`26:30`

Hope's radio crackled. "We're here," said Bergman, the driver. "There's quite a crowd. Get ready."

"Got it. Thanks, Bergman." Hope put the radio away and looked up at the clock. "Time to open the doors. Are you good to go?"

Audrey was still scared but also exhilarated. Yes, her friends in shops and restaurants probably weren't as stressed—but she bet they hadn't done anything as meaningful either. She was going to *save lives*.

"Ready," she said.

`25:40`

Hope unlocked the heavy steel door and pushed it open. Immediately the noise hit Audrey—the shouting and muttering and shuffling and jostling of a desperate crowd. Through the gap Audrey saw a collage of desperate faces. The volume rose to a roar as everyone fought to be closest to the door.

"There's so many," she said. "Why are they yelling?"

"They think there's not enough vaccine for everybody."

`25:00`

"Is there?"

Hope didn't reply.

Audrey grabbed the clipboard with the forms on it and held it up like a shield. Hope grabbed a man and a woman out of the crowd and dragged them both into the MTF. Then she shut the door again.

The woman was a stout, dark-haired lady in a T-shirt and shorts. Hope sat her down in a chair and presented her with a form and a pen. Apparently she was going to do admin stuff as well.

24:00

Audrey turned to the man. He was tall, with luminous blue eyes and a thick mane of blond hair. He wore a motorcycle jacket, a hiking backpack, leather pants, and boots that looked like they were designed for walks on the moon. One of his teeth was chipped to a jagged point.

"Hi," Audrey said. "I'm Audrey. I'll just get you to take a seat here and fill in this form, then we'll have you vaccinated in no time."

23:30

She felt like she had sounded very professional, but the man didn't look impressed.

"Yeah," he said, "that's not how this is going to work."

He pulled off his backpack and unzipped it.

"You're going to fill this up with the vaccine," he said, "and then I'm going to walk out of here."

23:05

"I don't understand," Audrey said, still smiling stupidly.

The man reached into his jacket and pulled out a small black cylinder with a yellow band around the middle and a ring hanging from the top.

"Now do you understand?" he said.

Audrey's brain completely froze up, like a computer running too many programs at once. The clash between the man's demand and what she had expected, the suddenness of it, had overwhelmed her.

The man pulled out the ring and held down the trigger of the grenade.

"I'm waiting," he said.

"Uh, Hope?"

Audrey looked over. Hope and her patient were already staring at the man in silent horror.

"It has a seven-second fuse," the man said. He released the trigger. Audrey recoiled.

The man squeezed the trigger again. "Now it has a five-second fuse," he said. "Trust me, you don't want to see it go boom. Fill up the bag. Now."

"Audrey, do as he says," Hope hissed.

"OK, OK," Audrey said hurriedly. "Take it easy. I'll just go get the syringes out of the fridge."

"Take the bag," the man advised. He didn't seem in the least bit anxious. Audrey wondered if he held up mobile treatment vehicles every day.

Probably. If there really wasn't enough of the vaccine to go around, this man could make a fortune selling it.

22:00

21:40

21:00

Clutching the bag in one hand, Audrey opened the fridge. The freezing air flooded out, sending swirls of mist along the floor. She grabbed shrink-wrapped syringes by the handful and started stuffing them into the backpack.

18:30

"Hurry up," the man said.

"I'm going as fast as I can," Audrey muttered.

Soon the backpack was full. Audrey cast a mournful look at the depleted shelves in the fridge. More than half their supplies were gone. Even if the man left without blowing them all up, hundreds of people outside would go untreated because of him.

Audrey turned back to the man. "Here," she said, thrusting the bag out.

He ignored her. He was looking out the window, his knuckles white around the grenade.

"Take it and go," Audrey said.

The man didn't react. He looked like she must have a moment ago—paralyzed.

Audrey followed his gaze—

And saw the car.

17:25

It was a white sedan with a cracked headlight and paint scraped off both sides. Audrey squinted so she could see the driver, a gaunt man with scruffy hair and a bright red beard.

No. Not a beard. His chin looked like it was smeared

82

with blood. People scrambled out of the way as the car mounted the curb and zoomed toward the MTF at full speed.

16:30

"Everybody down!" Audrey shrieked. She just had time to follow her own advice, diving under the nearest table, when the car smashed into the side of the MTF.

There was a mighty crash and the bottom half of the wall caved in. The whole world seemed to swing around as the MTF tipped over sideways. Audrey slammed into one of the walls as it became the floor. All the air whooshed out of her lungs and one of her ribs cracked with an audible *snap*.

16:10

The air filled with a hail of objects—papers, pens, wrapped syringes, rolls of tape and bandages, chairs, and even people. In a blur of leather and blond hair, the man flew across the room and banged into the wall. The desk Audrey cowered under was bolted to the wall and shielded her from most of the debris, but it couldn't block out the deafening racket.

15:50

When she opened her eyes, the MTF had settled on its side. The wall above her was a lumpy wreck. The wall below was awash with detritus.

As her eyes focused, she saw the grenade lying next to her. The man had dropped it in the chaos.

Audrey wasted a precious second staring at it before she came to her senses. How many seconds had it been?

She grabbed the grenade and held the trigger down.

One, two, three, four, five.

Nothing exploded.

She let out a shaky breath and stood up, holding the grenade in one hand. The surface had a papery texture. It was hard to believe something so light could do so much damage. But she didn't doubt that it was real. There had been something about the look on the man's face when he pulled the pin. And if she wasn't imagining it, the thing *smelled* explosive too.

Hope lay sprawled on the floor, unmoving. Her patient was facedown beside her. Audrey wanted to help them, but she had to deal with the grenade first.

14:50 There was no way to get it out of the MTF. The door couldn't be opened since it was facing the ground. The window above Audrey was out of reach, hadn't broken in the crash, and wasn't designed to open.

Audrey rummaged around in the debris until she found a roll of tape. She peeled off a strip with her teeth and wound it around and around and around the grenade, fixing the trigger in place. Then she took a deep breath and let go.

The tape held. The grenade didn't explode.

13:40 She placed it gingerly on the floor and then ran over to Hope.

"Hope," she said. "Are you OK?"

"Uhhhhhhh." Hope's eyelids fluttered.

Audrey felt a little fear melt away. Hope was alive!

"Ugh *hnnnn*," Hope groaned.

12:10

Audrey touched her shoulder. "We're trapped in here. The MTF is on its side. What should we do?"

Hope's eyes opened, but it looked like she couldn't focus. "Gurruhhh," she said, and shut her eyes again. A purple bruise was already spreading across her forehead.

Audrey turned to the other woman, trying to remember if she had heard her name. She couldn't.

She touched her back. "Can you hear me?"

The woman didn't respond.

11:30

Audrey very carefully rolled her onto her side. The woman's nose looked like it was broken, and one of her arms was twisted at an unnatural angle. But she was breathing, and she had a pulse.

Audrey knew that real life wasn't like the movies. A blow to the head strong enough to knock someone out was a very serious injury. Hope and the other woman needed medical help right away. But how could they get out with the door facing the ground?

11:00

The robber—or terrorist, or whatever—lay face-down in the corner. Audrey didn't check him for life signs. She didn't want to go anywhere near him.

"Help!" she screamed. "Can anyone hear me?"

10:50 No response. Audrey shivered. Since the crash, there had been absolute silence from the world outside. Audrey had the uneasy feeling that the area might have been evacuated. Something about an overturned vehicle with a full fuel tank and a hundred live virus samples probably made people nervous. Plus, it was possible that someone outside knew about the grenade. Anyone who did would want to get as far away as possible.

Audrey pounded on the wall. "Hey! Is anyone there?"

She waited. But there was just silence from the other side.

Her phone was still at the hospital, where she had boarded the MTF. It had been a legal requirement that she leave it behind. She wasn't a doctor, but she would be meeting patients and would be exposed to confidential information. But Hope's radio was supposed to be useful in an emergency.

Audrey looked around for Hope's radio. Soon she found it—well, half of it. The other half was presumably somewhere in the debris. Useless.

09:30 She shivered again. It was freezing in here. And suddenly she realized why—the door to the walk-in fridge had come off its hinges. The engine was still running, so the fridge was now cooling the entire vehicle.

Audrey ran over to the fridge, looking for a way to shut it off. It was a walk-in, so she couldn't just unplug it. She searched the stainless steel walls for a power switch or a thermostat, but there was nothing. Just row after row of icy shelves, half of which were above her head, the other half beneath her feet. She dug through the fallen syringes, but there wasn't anything useful beneath them. The temperature must be controlled from the driver's cabin.

08:15

She and Hope wore thin nurses' scrubs. The unconscious woman was in a T-shirt and shorts. Having survived the grenade and the crash—not to mention the deadly virus sweeping the country—were they really going to freeze to death?

It was possible. With so many cases of the virus spreading over the city, emergency services could take a long time to arrive.

07:40

Blankets. Hope had showed her where to find them in case a patient fainted after the injection. The cupboard had been fixed to the wall—now the floor. Audrey ran over, lifted the cupboard door and snatched up the blankets. There were only two. She draped one over Hope and one over the mystery woman. The cold was more dangerous to them than it was to her.

She rubbed her bare arms. Clouds of condensation wreathed her head with every exhale. How long would it be until someone came to rescue them?

07:00   She walked over to the front of the MTF. Maybe the driver was still here. Perhaps he would be able to hear her through the wall.

She thumped on the barrier. "Hey! Bergman! Can you hear me?"

No answer. She hoped he was OK.

Hope's lips were going blue. Her veins stood out like spiderwebs on her neck. Audrey wrapped the blanket a little more tightly around her, aware of how pitifully thin it was.

She wasn't a doctor. Not yet. But she couldn't just sit here and watch these two women die. Not if there was something—anything—she could do to save them.

06:25   Her eyes fell on the grenade.

No, she told herself. *Too crazy. It nearly killed us all. But . . . perhaps it's the only thing that can save us.*

The fuel tank was at the front of the MTF—Bergman had filled it up on the way here. The walk-in fridge was at the back. She headed down there to take a look. If she set off the bomb inside, it might blow a hole in the wall through which they could escape. If not, it might at least destroy important components of the fridge and stop them all from freezing to death.

Or it could flash-fry everyone inside.

She tried not to think about that.

She would have liked to close the fridge door to muffle the blast. But if she could close the fridge door there wouldn't need to be a blast in the first place.

06:00

She picked up all the syringes and tossed them to the other end of the MTF. The vaccine was precious. With any luck it would survive the explosion. Then she lifted the fallen fridge door. It seemed to weigh a ton— she hoped that meant it was thick enough to be a useful shield. She dragged it, arms and spine aching, over to where the two women lay.

Then she went for the grenade.

05:05

It took her a minute to find some scissors among the mess of junk. Her fingers trembled as she cut the tape. Was she really doing the right thing?

Maybe not. But surely doing nothing wasn't the right thing either.

She propped the fridge door up so the two women were sheltered behind it. She cowered beside them, the grenade clenched in one sweaty hand.

04:30

This was the most important throw of her life. If she missed the doorway, the grenade could bounce back and blow them all to pieces. Maybe it would do that even if she didn't miss.

She hesitated for the longest time. It was like standing on the high diving board at the swimming pool, trying to work up the courage to step into the void thirty-five feet below.

Come on, she told herself. *Just do it!*

04:10 She threw the grenade. Then with a little squeak of terror she ducked behind the fridge door.

Nothing happened.

Audrey waited, her heart in her mouth. What had gone wrong? Had it landed on its trigger, suspending the fuse? Or had it been a fake grenade after all? Or had it—

04:00 *BOOM!*

The fridge door hit her like a stampeding bull. She felt herself scream but couldn't hear it over the world-destroying blast. Super-heated air rushed past her, burning all the hairs off her arms. Debris rained down on her, sharp edges pricking her skin. She was blinded by the light. It was as though she'd tried to take a photograph of her own eyeball with the flash on.

Soon all she could hear was the shrill ringing in her ears. She blinked furiously, trying to get her vision back. But even when her sight returned, she couldn't see much. She was lying facedown.

03:30 She tried to get up. But she couldn't move at all. Her arms and legs wouldn't obey her.

A chill ran up her spine. *Oh no*, she thought. *I'm paralyzed!*

Then she realized the fridge door was lying on her back. With a mighty heave, she rolled sideways and it slid off, hitting the floor with a clang.

03:00

The MTF was full of acrid smoke. It stung her eyes and tickled the inside of her nostrils. She could hardly see.

But her ears were already recovering, and she could hear something. A distant siren. It was the first sound she had heard from outside the MTF since the door closed.

She put her hands under Hope's armpits and dragged her toward where the fridge used to be. Hope's feet skittered across the shrink-wrapped junk all over the floor.

What was once the fridge doorway was now a charred wreck. The closer Audrey got, the louder the outside world became. She could hear a howling wind, a squawking bird, and the distant drone of traffic.

02:30

And now she could see daylight. She had hoped to create a hole wide enough to crawl through, but the grenade had blown the whole wall out. Coughing and stumbling, she dragged Hope out into the street. The square was devoid of people and cars, but the sirens were getting louder. Hopefully they were for her.

Audrey hauled in a lungful of clean air and pushed back into the smoke to get the other woman. Syringes cracked under her feet and bled the precious vaccine into their plastic wrap. She wondered if the ones she hadn't stepped on were still useful.

01:50

She almost tripped over the woman, who made a weak groan that sounded like the air escaping from a soccer ball. Audrey pulled her carefully out of the MTF and into the sunshine.

She emerged just in time to see two ambulances screech to a halt next to the overturned vehicle. Paramedics jumped out and ran toward the two prostrate women. Someone shouted something at Audrey.

"Huh?" she said.

"Are you injured?" the paramedic said again. He was difficult to hear over the ringing that still filled Audrey's head.

"I'm OK, I think," she said. "Cuts and bruises. Help the others."

"They're being taken care of," the paramedic said, shining a light in her eyes. He was a short guy with a round, friendly face and stubble on his upper lip. "Is anyone else in the vehicle?"

"Yeah," Audrey said. "A criminal. I think he's dead. But be careful with his body. He might have more grenades."

The paramedic tried not to look alarmed and `00:25` failed. He turned to the hole in the side of the MTF. "Where is he?"

"He's right—" Audrey turned around, and screamed.

The smoke had cleared.

The bomber was gone. `00:00`

INFERNO

The smell was faint, but it woke Liliana up. It lingered in the night air like the last traces of a bad dream.

Art supplies, she thought. *That's what it smells like. Paint and charcoal.*

She peeled the covers off her sweaty legs and sat up. The air-conditioning didn't stand a chance against the summer heat. Even the floor was warm beneath her toes.

She had dreamed she was in a misty forest filled with stunted trees. She had seen a fox walking on its hind legs, staggering from side to side as though poisoned. She hid behind a twisted shrub, but the fox pulled the leaves back with its withered claws and fixed a bronze eye on her.

"Run, Liliana," it said.

Liliana rubbed her eyes. If she went back to sleep she would slip straight back into the nightmare. Time for a cup of chamomile tea—and to see if she could get rid of whatever was making that smell.

She got up, stretched her arms toward the old

glow-in-the-dark star stickers on the ceiling, and then padded along the carpet to the kitchen. She was especially quiet as she passed Mom and Dad's door, although she wasn't sure they were home yet. They had gone to the police station—apparently something had been stolen from one of their safety deposit boxes. They had left so quickly that the lamp was still on the living room floor where Dad had knocked it over while he was vacuuming.

`26:30`

Once upon a time she would have jumped into bed with them, no matter what time of night, to feel safe after a bad dream. Sometimes she had even pretended she'd had a nightmare just so they would let her sleep between them. She kind of missed those days. Her friends at school were always fighting over who could act the most grown up, but to Liliana, getting older seemed like a pain in the neck.

The kitchen was as ultra-modern as the rest of the apartment. A touchscreen controlled the oven. The fridge was connected to the internet and automatically kept the shopping list up to date. Liliana didn't turn on the light. The city skyline, shining bright against the moonless sky, was enough to illuminate the kettle and the contents of the pantry.

`25:50`

A ringing sound shattered the silence. It wasn't all that loud—the soundproofing was very good, at least on the upper floors—but it made Liliana jump.

It was probably the idiots down on the seventh floor accidentally setting off the fire alarm again. They often burned things in their microwave in the middle of the night. Liliana had heard that they struggled to tell the difference between seconds and minutes on the control panel.

25:00 She hoped they wouldn't have to evacuate the building while they waited for the fire department to switch off the alarm. Again. Perhaps she should be making her tea in a thermos rather than a mug.

She filled the kettle with water and switched it on. The blue light that usually flared up remained dark. *A power outage? Seriously?*

24:30 Liliana groaned, leaning against the wall. She had school tomorrow. She needed to sleep. She couldn't afford to spend all night standing outside—tealess—waiting for someone to switch off the alarm.

She turned her bleary eyes to the window—

And frowned.

The glass seemed to be fogged up. The lights of the city were diffused outward, blurry through the gray glaze. It was as though someone had smeared eggs on the window—this had happened once at the restaurant where Liliana worked on the weekends.

But the apartment was nine stories above the

ground. How could anyone throw an egg up here?

It wasn't until she got right up against the glass that she realized what was really going on. The fog wasn't on the glass at all—it was in the air outside.

The smell that awakened her wasn't charcoal. It was smoke.

She looked down and gasped. The street below was lit up by a flickering orange glow. In the windows of the shops opposite she could see the reflection of her apartment building.

It was on fire. The whole bottom level was consumed by a hungry blaze.

Liliana felt dizzy. She stumbled away from the window.

23:20

"Mom!" she screamed. "Dad!"

No answer from her parents' bedroom.

She ran, stumbling through the dark, her sleepiness washed away by terror. She crashed into her parents' door, fumbled with the handle and burst in.

"MomDadwakeupquick!" she blurted. "The building's on fire!"

22:30

There was no reply—because the bed was empty. Mom and Dad must not have gotten home from the police station yet. They were safe. But Liliana was alone.

She ran back to her room, ripped her phone off the

charger, and dialed 911. Before she hit call she realized that her phone was in flight mode—she always did that before she went to bed. She went into settings, turned flight mode off, and swiped back to the call screen. Then she remembered that her phone would probably call emergency services even when it was in flight mode.

Panic made people do dumb things, she knew. She had already wasted several seconds.

22:00 Before she had time to dial again, a message flashed up. She had eleven missed calls, all from her mother.

Somehow this scared her more than the smoke. Even more than the warmth coming up through her feet. Her heart was pounding.

She called her mother back.

21:50 The phone rang for about a second and a half before her Mom picked up.

"Liliana!" Mom screeched, so loud the phone crackled.

"Mom!"

"Where are you?"

21:30 "I'm—" Her heart broke. Her parents were probably desperately hoping that she was anywhere but here. "I'm at home."

Her mother—usually the calmest person in the world, especially when she was angry—screamed.

Her voice cracked, and she took a breath and screamed again. It sounded like she was being burned alive.

"Mom, where are you? Mom?" Liliana had to repeat the question three times before her mother responded.

"They won't let us in," she sobbed. "We're right outside, honey, but we can't get through!"

20:00

Liliana could hear Dad arguing with someone in the background. She opened the curtains and peered down, as if seeing her parents would make her safe. But two fire trucks and three ambulances had arrived. The red and blue lights were all she could see through the roiling smoke. It looked like a rock concert down there.

"What do I do?" Liliana asked. "Mom! What do I do?"

Mom didn't respond in words. She sounded as though she were being strangled.

19:30

The blaze below looked apocalyptic. Liliana wouldn't be able to get out that way, not until the firefighters subdued the flames. By the time that happened, she might already be dead from smoke inhalation. She had learned in school that almost no one died from the flames themselves. It was usually the smoke that killed people.

She wondered if it hurt, or if it just felt like going to sleep.

18:35

Liliana left the call connected—she was afraid that if she hung up, she might not be able to get through to her mother a second time. She walked from one end of the apartment to the other like a caged wolf. If she couldn't get out of the building, what could she do?

17:20

Maybe she could seal up the apartment so no smoke got in. She ran into the bathroom and grabbed the biggest towel she could find. She soaked it in the sink—at least the water was still running—and then rolled it into a tube. She carried it, dripping, all the way to the front door and jammed it underneath.

Would that stop the smoke from coming in around the edges? Maybe not, but it would help. She wet another towel in the bathroom, rolled it up, shut herself in her bedroom, and stuffed the towel under the door.

Now there were two barriers between her and the deadly smoke. Liliana had to hope that would be enough. She paced back and forth in front of the bed. How long before the firefighters had everything under control?

15:30

She was just starting to wonder if she should have shut herself in the bathroom instead when there was a *snap*. She swiveled around to face the window. A jagged crack had appeared in the glass, splitting the pane in two. As she watched, another crack branched out from the first.

Horrified, she scampered away from the window. It must be the heat from the fire below.

Soon the glass would shatter, leaving her bastion to fill with smoke.

15:00

She grabbed her supplies and fled from the bedroom. The bathroom would be no good either—there was a small frosted-glass window in there. Her parents had fallen in love with the apartment because every room had a window, all facing north. It seemed ridiculous that this very feature might kill her.

She would have to leave the apartment. But she couldn't go down to the ground floor.

So she'd have to make a break for the roof.

14:40

No ceiling above her head to hold down the smoke. Nothing flammable around her. Assuming the building itself didn't collapse—and it wouldn't, would it?—she would be safe until help came.

The phone was still on. "Mom," Liliana said. "Can you hear me?"

"Sweetie! What's going on?"

"I have to get out of the apartment before the smoke is too thick. I'm going to try to get to the roof."

14:20

"No, stay where you are! The firefighters will come and get you after they've put out the fire."

"I can't wait that long. Soon I won't be able to breathe.

Just let them know I'll be waiting on the roof."

"Liliana—"

"I love you," she said. "You and Dad. Tell him, OK?"

She hung up before the tears reached her eyes.

A flannel shirt hung from a rail in the bathroom. She grabbed it and soaked it in the sink. Then she ran to the front door.

13:00 Maybe it wouldn't be so bad out there. The fire was still several stories below her, she was pretty sure. Just in case, she mapped out the route in her head. Through the door, turn right, run all the way to the end, turn left, and she would be at the entrance to the stairs. After that, it should be an easy climb to the roof.

She took a deep breath and clamped the flannel over her mouth and nose to keep out the smoke. Then she pulled the door open.

12:30 A billowing fog of acrid soot hit her immediately. As she stepped into the corridor and pulled the door shut behind her, a thousand flecks of icy water stung her cheeks and hair. The sprinklers were on. With the roaring of the fire from somewhere below, it was like being outside in a thunderstorm.

She couldn't see anything through the smoke. The heat baked her eyeballs so she shut them. The clanging of the fire alarm made it hard to think.

Right, then all the way to the end of the hall, then left, she told herself. She staggered out the door and then crashed straight into the wall. She had turned too late. She stumbled back, disoriented.

She didn't have much time. If she breathed in, she was dead. Liliana steeled herself and ran through the black fog, keeping one hand on the wall so she didn't get lost. The wet carpet was spongy beneath her bare feet.

12:00

Soon she was at the end of the corridor. She turned left and fumbled her way across the wall until she found the door to the fire stairs. It didn't have a handle—just a crash bar. She pushed it open.

She noticed that the metal was hot but registered it too late. The door swung open and a whirlwind of fire roared in front of her. The flames were in the stairwell somehow, as though someone had spilled gasoline on the stairs or filled the stairwell with flammable gas.

11:30

As the door opened, the oxygen rushed from the corridor into the stairwell, feeding the fire. The hungry flames billowed up as a deadly wind rushed up behind Liliana, trying to push her toward them. She fought the current, pushing back so hard she overbalanced and fell onto the carpet, already dry and charred beneath her. The heat scraped her skin. Sparks filled the air like fireflies.

11:20

She couldn't do this. There was no way up *or* down.

She had to go back to the apartment.

Liliana had dropped the flannel in her panic. She grasped randomly at the floor until she found it again and clamped it over her face. Then she clambered to her feet and ran away from the stairwell, the fire chasing her.

11:00 The smoke was like squid ink. When she collided with the apartment door, it seemed to take her a thousand years to find the handle.

She tried to turn it. Locked.

No! She rattled the handle desperately. There was no air left in her lungs. She was sure she'd left the door unlocked.

So this must be the wrong door. She staggered farther up the corridor, dizzy and blind, until she found another one. This time the handle turned.

10:30 She burst into her apartment, slammed the door shut, and ripped the flannel off her face. She took a deep, desperate breath, and promptly threw up on the floor. It was partly the fear, partly the smoke she had inhaled.

Her expedition had been costly. The apartment had more smoke in the air than before, and now the fire had spread to the corridor outside. Even if the sprinklers managed to suppress it, she still had to deal with the glass.

After rubbing her aching eyes she saw that the `09:35` living room window had a giant spiderweb of cracks. One small piece had fallen out or melted away. The wind roared outside.

She fell to her knees on the tiles. *I can't stay here or I'll die. I can't leave or I'll die. It's hopeless.*

Liliana stared through the splintered glass at the city, the buildings and water towers and telephone lines silhouetted against the fire-lit sky— `08:45`

Telephone lines.

She had an idea.

Maybe it was the carbon dioxide getting to her brain, but it seemed like she could survive this. If she was brave, and just a little crazy.

Her parents' new vacuum cleaner was still on the floor where Dad had left it after the phone call about the safe deposit box. It was a tremendous backpack-style model, designed to clean office buildings, not small apartments. It was ludicrously over-powered, and not just when it came to sucking up dust. When Dad pushed the *retract cable* button, the power cord zoomed back into the device so fast that it knocked over a lamp. Mom had tried to convince him to return it to the store. `07:50`

Liliana carried the vacuum cleaner back into the kitchen. She would need something to weigh down the other end of the power cable. She tied one end to the handle of the electric kettle. That would have to do.

Back in the living room, she picked up the fallen lamp and slammed the steel base into the window. The cracked glass shook but didn't shatter. She swung the lamp again. Since the window had been tough enough to withstand the first blow, perhaps it wouldn't break under the heat either. Perhaps she could stay here. But by the time this occurred to her, the stool was already in motion, and when the impact came, it smashed the glass to pieces.

07:00 The momentum of the stool nearly pulled Liliana out the window. She let go just in time and teetered on the edge as she watched the stool plummet thirty, forty, fifty feet, surrounded by a halo of shards. It hit the distant asphalt with a hideous crack, legs flying off in all directions.

If the fall did that to a metal bar stool, what would it do to Liliana?

06:30 There was no time to dwell on that. Smoke was leaking in from around the door and wafting through the empty window frame. She had to go right now.

According to the label on the side of the vacuum, the power cable was fifty feet long. The telephone line across the street looked thirty or forty feet away. *Close enough,* she hoped.

// INFERNO //

She swung the power cord like a lasso. The kettle `06:05` was still tied to the end—it swept around and around, gaining speed with every swing. Liliana took aim at the telephone line and let go.

The kettle whipped out into the void but fell short of the line. It swung down into the flames below the window instead. When Liliana pulled it back up, the rubber base was slightly melted and the metal lid glowed like a stovetop coil.

This is insane, she thought. *I can't do this.* `04:55`

But she knew she didn't have a choice. This wasn't a nightmare she could hide from in her parents' bed. This was real life. Do or die.

She swung the kettle again. This time it sailed over the distant telephone line, wrapping the power cord around it.

Liliana tugged the cord with her sweaty hands. She thought it would take her weight. `04:30`

Smoke was pouring in from all directions. Under the door, through the window, from the other rooms. Liliana had planned to tie the vacuum cleaner to the doorhandle and climb across the power cord to safety. But now there was no time. If she didn't get out of here right now, she would asphyxiate.

She pulled the vacuum cleaner onto her back, tightened the shoulder straps and buckled them together over her chest. She stood on the edge, teetering over the sheer drop into the roaring flames—

03:35 Then she pushed the *retract cable* button.

She had worried that the mechanism wouldn't be strong enough, but it sucked her out the window immediately. The heat hit her like a wall. She squeezed her eyes shut as she plummeted through the cloud of smog, her stomach churning. Just when she thought she must be about to slam into the ground, the cord went taut and she swung outward, hurtling across the road to the buildings on the other side. She whipped past the telegraph pole and found herself flying upward like a kid on a tire swing.

03:10 She slowed down and down until she was hanging in the air, motionless, about twenty feet above the ground. Then she was falling again. She clung desperately to the power cable as the ground rushed up to meet her—

But the cable went taut again, swinging her back toward the blazing building—

And just in time, a chunk broke off the vacuum cleaner. The power cable flicked away and Liliana was free. Her bare feet skidded across the road hard enough to draw blood and she tumbled over forward, scraping her palms and knees. Then all was still. She lay facedown on the warm asphalt, listening to the pop and crackle of the flames.

It had worked. She was out.

Gloved hands grabbed her and hauled her up. She found herself slung over the shoulder of a burly firefighter as he carried her and the vacuum back toward the cordon.

"I'm OK," she said. "I can walk."

He ignored her, which was probably good, since she wasn't sure it was the truth. Behind them another window exploded in the heat. Broken glass rained down on the road.

The firefighter squeezed between the crowd barriers and deposited Liliana on the ground. He cut through the shoulder straps of the vacuum with some kind of blade. Liliana gasped as the tension across her chest was released.

"Can you hear me?" the firefighter asked.

Liliana nodded.

"Are you hurt?"

"Just my feet," she said. "And my hands."

"OK." The firefighter pointed to one of the nearby ambulances. "The paramedics will check you out and clear you to go."

Go where? Liliana wondered. *My home just went up in flames.*

"Liliana!" a voice screamed.

02:40

01:55

01:30

00:45 Liliana whirled out. "Mom! I—"

She didn't have time to finish the sentence before she was swept into a hug. Her face was pressed against her mother's chest, and she felt kisses rain down on the top of her head. She felt her father's arms wrap around the two of them.

"It's OK," he said. "It's OK."

Liliana closed her eyes as she was squashed
00:00 between her parents, safe at last.

FLYRUS

"**W**ill this hurt?" Tony asked.   30:00

"What are you, five?" Shane kicked a stone into the gutter and pumped his fist in the air as it disappeared into a stormwater drain. His skateboard was tucked casually under one arm.

"A five-year-old wouldn't think to ask," Tony said, determined not to be provoked. "Not until the needle came out. I just want to be prepared."   29:40

"They'll tell you it feels like 'a little pinch,'" Shane said, "because that sounds nicer than saying it feels like getting stabbed in the arm."

"Thanks, Shane. You've been a big help."

"Of course, it feels a whole lot better than catching the flyrus."

"Which is why I'm getting the vaccine," Tony said.

"Just imagine," Shane continued. "Coughing up your lungs while your eyeballs melt and your brains leak out your ears . . ."

"The flyrus doesn't do that."

"Yes it does. I heard it on the radio."

Tony's parents worked at the hospital. He knew there were things they didn't tell him because they thought he was too young, but they had explained the flyrus very thoroughly.

"You're making that up," he said.

28:00

"Am not."

"Are too. Look, there's the vaccination center."

The vaccination center was just a white shipping container on a semitrailer parked in the town square. Tony had asked his parents why hospitals weren't immunizing people, and his mom said the disease was too contagious. If everyone in the city went to the hospital to get their vaccinations, half of them would get infected just waiting in line.

27:30

The truck hadn't opened its doors yet, but it was already surrounded by a crush of people. Tony swallowed. If just one of those people were already infected, the disease could ripple through the crowd.

He wished his parents were here. But they were doctors, and they were needed at the hospital. He would just have to trust them when they had told him the infected would be easy to spot and avoid.

The appearance of the first few patients—staggering groggily, blood around their lips—led some to announce that the zombie apocalypse had arrived. People had barricaded their doors and plastered their windows with newspaper. A cure had been developed quickly, but the vaccine took longer, and it felt like the whole country had gone crazy.

27:00

"Are you coming, or what?" Shane demanded.

"Yeah, yeah." Tony followed him into the crowd.

The line wasn't much of a line. It was more like a winding family tree, splitting off in several directions with everyone glaring at one another. Everybody seemed to be waiting for everyone else to push in.

Shane and Tony joined the back of the line, or one branch of it, just in time to see the doors open. Tony got a brief glimpse of the inside of the shipping container— ultra-modern, ultra-sterile—before two people were hauled inside and the doors shut again.

26:00

"How long do you think it takes?" Tony asked.

"Five minutes per person," Shane said. He spoke with absolute confidence, but Tony knew from experience that Shane often regarded his own guesses as facts. They were friends largely because their parents had gone to college together, and while Tony didn't like Shane's flaws, at least he was aware of them. He'd rather hang out with Shane than with the other kids at school, whose defects were unknown.

25:30

But maybe Shane was right. If so, it would only take them two—Tony did a quick headcount—or maybe three hours to reach the front of the line, have their shots, and get out of here. After that they would have their immunization certificates and could go back to doing normal things. School, basketball, going out. Those things weren't allowed for people who hadn't yet been treated with the vaccine. And Tony was getting the vaccine on day one. He was kind of looking forward to being the only one out and about. Sitting alone in a movie theater, walking through a deserted supermarket . . .

23:45 "This is pointless," Shane said. "Once everyone's immunized, whoever designed the flyrus will just release a slightly different version of it. There goes our immunity. Until they're caught, vaccinations are a waste of time."

23:30 "What makes you think anyone designed the flyrus?" Tony asked.

"It's obvious. Swine flu could make the jump to humans naturally, because humans and pigs are really similar. You can even transplant a pig's heart into a person. Bird flu works too—birds aren't mammals, but they're warm-blooded, like people. But flies are insects. There's no way that the same virus should be able to infect us and them. Not unless it was engineered."

It was actually a pretty well-reasoned argument, by Shane's standards.

"But why would anyone do that?"

"Lots of reasons. Maybe it's an attack from another country. Maybe it's environmentalists who want to wipe out humanity. Maybe—"

23:00

"I don't think environmentalists want humans to be extinct. They just want to make sure we still have somewhere to live in fifty years."

"That's what they want you to think," Shane said. "But most environmental threats are human-made. What better way to protect nature than to . . ."

Tony had stopped listening. He was watching a car on the nearby road. The presence of the car itself wasn't unusual, although the outbreak had noticeably reduced traffic. But the car was moving erratically, swiping from side to side as though overtaking other drivers who weren't there.

"Do you see that?" Tony said.

"The question is, how quickly would the earth recover?" Shane said, ignoring him. "I think after twenty years—"

"Shane, look."

22:20

The car was driving faster and faster. After a few erratic turns, it was facing the treatment truck and still accelerating. The engine howled as it mounted the curb.

"Look out!" Tony yelled. He grabbed Shane's arm

and pulled him away from the truck as the car zoomed toward it.

SMASH! The sound hit Tony like a physical barrier as the car slammed into the side of the shipping container. The truck groaned like a hungry giant's belly as it tipped, slowly at first but gaining speed as it overbalanced. The nearest people barely managed to get out from underneath as it crashed to the ground with a sound like a thunderclap.

21:30

No one had been crushed, but the air filled with screams. Some people ran away from the toppled truck, others ran toward it. Shane was staring at the carnage with a mixture of fear and delight. He was always making up horror stories, perhaps because nothing interesting happened in his real life, and now one was unfolding right in front of him.

20:50

Tony pulled his arm. "Come on!"

"Where to?"

It seemed obvious to Tony. "To help the driver."

They ran around to the far side of the fallen truck. The car was resting six feet away, having bounced back after the impact. The front half was crumpled like a bag of potato chips. Frayed ribbons of rubber surrounded the blown-out tires. The driver was slumped forward into a bloodstained airbag.

20:30

Tony wrenched the door open. It came off its

hinges and hit the ground with a *thunk*. Little cubes of shatterproof glass fell out of the window frame.

"Can you hear me?" Tony asked. "Sir?"

The driver didn't respond.

Tony reached past him to unbuckle his seatbelt. The airbag looked like a pillow but was surprisingly firm, like a leather ottoman. Eventually he found the seatbelt and hit the release button.

19:40

Immediately the driver fell sideways. Tony caught him and wheezed under his weight. He was so heavy that his lifeless arm swung into Tony's chest with the force of a punch.

"You want to give me a hand?" he gasped.

"Not really," Shane said.

Tony lowered the unconscious man to the ground. His eyes were swollen shut with purple flesh. His face was smeared with blood.

18:50

Tony pressed his finger to the man's slippery neck. He couldn't find a pulse.

"Tony," Shane said. "I don't think you should touch him."

"His heart's stopped," Tony said, rolling up his sleeves. "He needs CPR."

"He's got the flyrus."

Tony froze. "How can you tell?"

"Look at the bruises around his eyes. Look at

the way he was driving."

"That doesn't mean anything," Tony said, trying to keep the doubt from his voice.

Then the man coughed.

18:20 Hot blood splashed Tony's face. He recoiled as the man coughed again, unleashing another spray of blood.

It was a classic symptom of the flyrus.

"No," Tony whispered.

The man's eyes opened a crack. They rolled to look at Tony and then they glazed over. When Tony moved, the eyes didn't follow him. The driver was dead.

Tony turned to see that Shane had already stepped back several feet.

"Don't come any closer," Shane said.

17:15 Other people were coming around the side of the fallen truck. They stared at the gruesome scene—the crushed car, the dead body, Tony all covered in blood.

"Shane," Tony said. "Please."

"Get back!" Shane yelled at him.

The bystanders looked from Shane to Tony.

"He's infected!" a young woman yelled.

A tall man swore and brandished an umbrella like a weapon. A heavyset guy picked up one of the car's fallen mirrors and held it up like a club. One by one, Tony watched the crowd turn into an angry mob.

"I need to get to a hospital," Tony said. "To get tested."

"Then go!" shrieked a woman clutching a paving stone. "Get out of here!"

16:30

"I'll never make it on foot." The treatment was only effective if it was administered within twenty minutes of exposure. Tony was ten miles from the nearest hospital.

"Not our problem," the man with the umbrella growled.

To Tony's horror, even Shane had picked up his skateboard and was wielding it like a baseball bat.

"Shane," Tony said.

"Get back," Shane said. "I mean it."

Tony didn't move. "Please. I'll never make it to the hospital alone."

16:00

Shane swung the skateboard at him.

Tony was too shocked to even duck. The board hit him in the chest, knocking the air out of his lungs. He wrapped his arms around it so Shane couldn't take another swing.

15:40

Shane let go of the board and stumbled back, perhaps realizing how close he was to a potentially infected person. He turned and fled. So did the rest of the crowd. They ran as though Tony were a nuclear warhead.

Tony stood in the deserted square, dazed. He couldn't believe how quickly the people had become animals. How Shane had turned on him without a moment's hesitation.

He circled around the toppled semitrailer. Maybe the people inside could help him, or he could help them. But there didn't seem to be a way in. The driver of the truck was nowhere to be seen.

15:00 Too late, Tony realized he was in another kind of danger. *Whumpff.* Smoke leaked out from under the hood of the crashed car. If the flames reached the gas tank, it would explode.

Tony ran. His heart felt like it would burst. The wind was freezing on his hot skin. After two blocks he collapsed, exhausted.

The streets were deserted. No cars, no pedestrians, no anything. The buses weren't running. How could he get to the hospital to get tested?

13:50 He still had Shane's skateboard. But he was at the bottom of a valley and the hospital was at the top of a hill. The board wouldn't help much.

He would have to call an ambulance to take him. But would it arrive in time? He whipped out his cell and dialed 911.

13:30 The phone rang twice before a recorded message cut in. "All our operators are currently busy. Please stay on the line. All our operators are currently busy. Please . . ."

// FLYRUS //

Tony listened to the message over and over, panic growing in his belly until he couldn't take it anymore. How long would it take for someone to pick up? When they did, how long before the ambulance arrived? Add another five minutes to drive to the hospital, five minutes to get admitted, another five to get tested . . .

An explosion of coughs bent his body in half. He hacked a gob of spit into the gutter and gasped for breath.

It could have just been something caught in my throat, he thought. *I often cough after I run. It's not necessarily the flyrus.*

He opened the camera app in his phone and took a selfie. When the picture appeared on the screen, he gasped.

Two dark rings encircled his eyes. He looked like he was wearing makeup.

A surge of bile rose up his throat. He choked it back down. There was no need to get the test. He definitely had the flyrus. And if he wasn't treated soon, he would die a horrible death.

The call was still connected. "All our operators are currently busy. Please stay on the line."

The city must be full of sick people, or people who thought they were sick. There couldn't possibly be enough ambulances for everybody. There weren't even enough operators to talk to all the callers.

The growl of approaching tires echoed around the street. Tony turned to see a hatchback zooming toward him. He stepped out onto the road, waving his arms eagerly.

12:00

"Hey!" he yelled. "I need help!"

The car slowed. The side window rolled down, revealing the driver—a young woman with thick glasses and a neck tattoo.

The driver looked at the blood on Tony's face and the dark circles around his eyes. Her mouth fell open. She swerved around him and sped up, rocketing away out of sight.

11:30

Tony felt tears sting the corners of his eyes. No one would help him. No one was willing to even be near him. He was going to die alone.

The recorded message was still going. Surely it was too late now—even if someone picked up the phone and sent an ambulance there was no way it would arrive in time to save him.

11:20

He hung up and called his mom.

"Hi, you've called Dana," her voicemail said. "I can't come to the phone right now, but—"

Tony ended the call and tried his dad instead.

"I'm unable to take your call at the moment," his

father's voice said, "but if you leave your name, number, and a brief message, I'll get back to you as soon as I can."

They would both be busy at the hospital.

10:50

"Dad," Tony said. "Something happened on my way to get vaccinated. An accident. I think I have the flyrus. I'm really sorry." His voice wobbled. "If I don't make it, I just want you to know that I love you and Mom, and thank you for everything, and take care of each other. I had a good life, and I know I was lucky to have parents like you."

He couldn't think of anything else to say, so he hung up. Tears streaming down his face, he called Mom again just so he could listen to her voice on the answering machine.

10:05

"Hi, you've called Dana. I can't come to the phone right now, but if you leave a message, I'll call you right back."

Tony was about to leave his mom a message when he heard it.

A siren.

09:55

Could be police. Could be a fire truck.

Could be an ambulance. With a life-threatening illness sweeping the city, that was the most likely.

He started running toward the source of the noise. It was downhill, so he jumped on Shane's skateboard. He rolled down the empty road, keeping one foot on the board and pounding the concrete with the other for extra speed. Soon he was racing through an alley at a reckless pace, swerving around Dumpsters and abandoned shopping carts, the wind buffeting his hair as he struggled to stay balanced. It would be ironic if in his desperation to get help he fell off the skateboard and broke his neck.

08:00 He burst out of the alley onto a main street just in time to see an ambulance appear at the far end. It turned toward him, siren howling, and hurtled closer and closer.

"Hey!" Tony shouted, waving his arms. "I need help! Hey!"

07:45 The ambulance must have had a more urgent mission. It ignored him completely, accelerating up the street until Tony had to scoot backward to avoid being crushed beneath the wheels.

There was a fifty-fifty chance it was headed to the hospital.

Those odds were good enough to be worth risking his life. So, as the ambulance swept past—

07:00 Tony grabbed hold of the tow bar.

The sudden increase in speed nearly pulled his arm out of its socket. He crouched low, holding onto the skateboard with his other hand so it wasn't pulled out from under him. The tiny wheels roared along the asphalt with a sound like a giant zipper being undone. **06:55**

It had been hard to balance before, but that was nothing compared to now. The board fishtailed left and right under Tony's feet. It was like trying to stand on an electric eel. Tiny flecks of black grit kicked up from under the ambulance's tires.

If the ambulance driver knew Tony was clinging to the back of the vehicle, they didn't show it. The ambulance swerved around a corner, and he nearly tumbled sideways off the board. **06:20**

This was the most dangerous thing he had ever done. Mom and Dad had treated several kids with cracked skulls from trying to ride behind cars. Some of them had even died. And Tony didn't even have a helmet. If Mom and Dad found out he had done this—and he somehow survived the journey *and* the flyrus—they would murder him themselves.

The shrieking siren was driving him crazy. His eardrums felt like overripe fruit about to burst. The noise was making him dizzy. **06:00**

Or maybe it wasn't the noise. He was starting to feel really ill now. The air seemed to be freezing even though it was a bright, sunny day. His sinuses felt like they were packed with glue. He could hardly swallow because his throat was so constricted.

The virus was killing him. He didn't have much

time left. He tightened his grip on the tow bar. The metal was slippery in his sweaty hands. If he lost his grip, he was dead. The road was a blur beneath the wheels of the skateboard.

05:35 And suddenly it was getting harder to hold on. The road was sloped upward now, so Tony's arms and hands were fighting gravity.

Wait. Uphill?

As the ambulance turned another corner, Tony saw it. The hospital, perched atop the hill like a medieval castle. Luck had been on his side for once. He was nearly there.

But he was so tired. His brain felt like it was made of steel wool. When he looked down at his straining arms he saw that the bruising had spread. His veins stood out like tattoos.

04:30 The ambulance rocketed up the winding road. Tony felt like he was on a roller coaster. He couldn't hold on anymore.

I'm sorry, Mom, he thought. *Sorry, Dad—*

04:10 The ambulance stopped so suddenly that he slammed into the back of it. His brain quivered like jelly inside his skull, the world around him sparkling at the edges. He fell onto the road and lay flat on his back, unable to move, staring up at the blue sky. Shane's skateboard rolled away back down the hill.

// FLYRUS //

The two paramedics circled around to the back of the ambulance to open the doors and froze when they saw him.

03:50

"How did you get there?" one demanded. The other looked up, as though Tony might have fallen from the sky.

Tony didn't have the strength to respond. He felt like his arms and legs were bound in iron chains.

"Take him inside," one of the paramedics said. "Quick. I'll get the other one out."

The other paramedic picked Tony up without hesitation. He must have been vaccinated—he didn't look at all scared of the flyrus. The world swirled around Tony again and he tried not to puke as the paramedic slung him over his shoulder and carried him through the front doors of the hospital.

03:00

The room was full of people—old, young, thin, fat. Some were pale, others were bleeding, but none looked as sick as Tony.

The paramedic hauled Tony over to the triage desk.

"No idea where this one came from," he told the receptionist. "Found him out front. Looks like the final stages of flyrus."

02:30

"Tony!" a voice shouted. A voice Tony had thought he'd never hear again.

Mom, he tried to say, but the word wouldn't come out.

"You know him?" the receptionist said. "You can fill out the admission paperwork."

01:50

"Later," Mom said. She was wearing scrubs, with a stethoscope dangling around her neck and a blue cap concealing her hair. She pushed a gurney toward the paramedic. "Put him on this."

The paramedic dumped Tony onto the gurney and ran back out to the ambulance. Mom pushed the gurney out of the waiting room and down a corridor onto a ward.

"You're going to be OK," she said. "I promise." Tony's eyes were blurred, but he thought his mother was crying.

00:35

The ward was full of other patients hooked up to IV drips with breathing masks on their faces. Mom rummaged in a cupboard, grabbed a shrink-wrapped syringe and rolled up Tony's sleeve.

"You might feel a little pinch," she said. But in fact, Tony didn't feel anything at all. He just lay there, holding his mother's hand as the cure entered his

00:00

bloodstream and began its work.

RUNAWAY TRAIN

Kelli-Anne stared at the sign.

FARE EVASION—IT'S A CRIME.

She knew the train cost money to run, and if one of the passengers rode for free the others wound up paying more. But she really, *really* needed to get home.

Her parents were expecting her, and if she wasn't at her house soon, they would call her. She wouldn't answer because her phone—and wallet—were in the bag that had just been snatched from her shoulder. Then her parents would panic, call the police, and instigate a statewide manhunt. It had been a year since the flyrus was eliminated, but they were still ultra-nervous whenever she went out on her own.

She looked left and right. The platform was deserted. No security guards, no cameras that she could see. It was just Kelli-Anne, the howling wind, and the cloudless sky. There wasn't even a turnstile to jump over—just a post with a screen for her to tap her rail pass on.

It would be so easy.

Light glinted off something approaching in the distance. A foghorn honked. The train was coming. It was now or never.

28:00 Kelli-Anne tapped her hand against the screen as though she were holding a rail pass, just in case there was a security camera she couldn't see. Then she ran onto the platform just as the train was pulling to a stop in front of it.

The doors whooshed open. Kelli-Anne cast a guilty look each way and boarded the train car.

She was the only passenger in the train car. The vinyl cushions gleamed stickily on the seats. A trapped moth fluttered from one end of the fluorescent light to the other. Words, probably obscene but completely illegible, were scratched into the plastic windows.

27:20 Kelli-Anne sighed and sat down on one of the seats as the train started rolling. Not only had she lost her wallet and her phone, she had lost her status as a law-abiding citizen.

She wondered if all criminals started out on the right side of the law until something made them violate their own moral code. Maybe the person who stole her bag had been desperate for a meal.

26:50 But no, it couldn't always be like that. She knew kids who downloaded movies and TV shows without paying for them, and it wasn't because anyone *forced* them to. They just didn't want to pay, or wait for the Blu-ray, or watch any of the million free things instead.

So she guessed there were two types of criminals—those who stole out of necessity, and those who took things because they simply felt entitled to them.

The wheels rattled under the carriage. Kelli-Anne swayed from side to side as the train rounded a gentle curve. When the train was full of people, all rocking in unison, she liked to pretend that they were dancing to the music in her headphones. It was no fun on her own. And her headphones were gone, like everything else in her bag.

`25:15`

Her favorite lip gloss? Gone. The autographed fantasy novel she had been reading? Gone. Her keys to her house, her locker, her bike lock? All gone.

She sighed and looked out the window at the daylight glaring down on the shipyards. The cranes were silhouetted against the distant coast like long-dead trees.

`24:55`

She could hear a faint voice. For a moment she thought it was her phone—maybe she hadn't disconnected the last call she was on—but then she remembered that she didn't have it with her.

Kelli-Anne turned around. No one in the seats behind her. Wondering if she was going crazy, she bent down to peer under the seats. Nobody hiding beneath them. She was definitely alone in the carriage.

24:00 Maybe someone was talking in the next car along. She craned her neck, peering through the walkway which joined the two carriages. She saw no one.

Kelli-Anne eyed the locked door that led to the motorman's compartment. He must be talking to himself—or on the phone to someone. It probably got pretty boring driving a train. No steering, no talking to passengers. Just the accelerator and the brake, and for all Kelli-Anne knew, the process was partly automated.

23:30 The voice stopped abruptly.

Kelli-Anne was just wondering what that meant when the voice came back, this time much louder, crackling over the PA system.

23:00 "The next station is Grandstand," the conductor said. He sounded flustered. Perhaps he had gotten caught up in his phone conversation and had forgotten that a stop was coming up. "This train will terminate at Grandstand. Please disembark the train."

The message was repeated twice more. Kelli-Anne frowned. This train was supposed to go all the way to Grenville, where her house was. Why was it stopping here? How was she going to get home?

The brakes hissed and whined. Kelli-Anne looked out the window at the approaching platform, a slab of concrete under garish lighting and a white-tile ceiling.

Two uniformed transit police were waiting on it.

Kelli-Anne felt the blood drain from her face. Were they here for her? Had someone seen her get on without paying?

22:05

She slunk down into her seat, low enough that they wouldn't see her through the window. What was she going to do? She'd seen transit officers confront people without tickets before. Sometimes they gave them a pass if they had a driver's license that proved they were from out of town, or something. But Kelli-Anne had no ID at all. What would they do to her?

She took another peek through the window. A few passengers were disembarking and wandering around the platform, heads high, searching for signs. Kelli-Anne guessed that they hadn't known the train was stopping here either.

21:00

The transit officers didn't get on board but they also didn't leave. They just stood there, sipping coffee and chatting. Kelli-Anne hoped they would move on before the train started moving in the other direction.

20:00

After a minute, another announcement came over the PA. "Doors closing," the conductor said. "Please stand clear."

Kelli-Anne was paralyzed. If she stayed on board, there was no telling where she might end up. But if she

19:40

got off and the police officers *were* there for her, then they would see her and maybe arrest her. How had this gotten so out of control so quickly?

She hesitated too long. The doors hissed closed.

Something rattled behind her. The conductor was opening his door. If he saw Kelli-Anne, he would throw her off the train. She scrambled under the seat and held her breath.

She saw the door open. The conductor's polished shoes clopped past her. He was talking on the phone.

19:00 "There must be a better way," he said.

Kelli-Anne could faintly hear the voice of the man on the other end of the line: "That's not your problem."

"I could lose my job," the conductor said. "*That's* my problem."

He walked all the way through the carriage and disappeared into the next one. Kelli-Anne guessed he was sweeping the train to make sure no one was on board.

She risked another peek out the window. The transit officers were still there. Waiting.

How was she going to get out of this?

She wished she had her phone so she could call her parents for advice or rescue. But if she had her **17:55** phone she wouldn't be in this mess in the first place.

The conductor reappeared. Kelli-Anne just had

time to duck out of sight before he swept into the carriage, still on the phone.

"That's not enough," he said. "I want double that."

The voice on the phone mumbled something.

"Easy for you to say. You don't have to leave everything behind and start over."

The voice said *something hundred thousand.*

17:30

The conductor hesitated for a moment. Then: "Fine."

Kelli-Anne squirmed under the seat. What was she listening to? Something very illegal, by the sound of it. If she were caught now, she might find herself in much worse trouble than getting handed over to the transit police.

The conductor disappeared back into the driver's compartment. He didn't close the door, which meant that Kelli-Anne had to stay hidden in case he looked back.

17:05

The train groaned as it started moving again. She had expected it to go back in the opposite direction, but it kept crawling farther along the track. Maybe she would get home after all.

She shrank back in alarm as one of the passenger doors slid open, revealing the wall of the tunnel as it slid by. The train was still moving very slowly, but seeing the tunnel roll past was unnerving. It was as though she had gone to the aquarium to watch the sharks and had suddenly realized there was no glass between her and them.

16:40 Obviously there had been some kind of malfunction. Did the conductor know?

16:30 No sooner had this thought crossed her mind than the conductor emerged from the driver's compartment and walked over to the door. Kelli-Anne expected him to pull out a wrench and start fiddling with the controls, but instead he stepped out into the tunnel and vanished.

Kelli-Anne gasped and ran over to the open door. She wanted to jump out after him—he couldn't have jumped, he must have fallen, he might be hurt—but the train was accelerating. She didn't have the courage to leap out, and every second she waited made it worse. The tunnel whirled past faster and faster. If she jumped now, she could break her legs or be crushed under the wheels.

15:15 It took a moment for the gravity of the situation to sink in. The conductor was gone. She was the only person on board a speeding train. She had no idea where it was going or how to stop it getting there.

She ran to the driver's compartment. The conductor had closed the door behind him, and there was no handle—just a keyhole. Kelli-Anne pounded on the door, just in case someone else was in there.

"Hey!" she shouted. "Can you stop the train? Hello?"

No response.

An emergency call button was mounted on the wall beside the passenger door. Kelli-Anne ran back over to it. A sign said USE OF THIS BUTTON EXCEPT IN EMERGENCIES WILL RESULT IN A FINE. Kelli-Anne ignored the sign and pushed the button.

`15:00`

The phone rang and rang and rang. With a sinking feeling, Kelli-Anne realized that it wasn't dialing out. She could hear the conductor's phone ringing in the driver's compartment.

`14:05`

No way off the train. No way to stop it. Or was there?

Her eyes fell on the neatly packaged fire blanket on the wall—and the extinguisher hanging beneath it. It looked heavy.

She picked the extinguisher up. It *was* heavy. According to the label it was packed with compressed CO_2. An alarm shrieked as it came off the wall, making her jump. The extinguisher slammed down on her foot and she yelped. Fortunately nothing exploded.

`13:30`

She carried the extinguisher over to the driver's compartment door and rammed the canister against the lock. The door rattled but didn't open. She swung again, harder. The lock didn't break, but a crack split the plastic coating on the door. Encouraged, Kelli-Anne hurled the canister with all the strength she could muster and it smashed a hole the size of a coffee cup through the door.

13:00   Kelli-Anne reached through the gap and fumbled for the handle on the other side. Shards of plastic and splintered wood scraped her forearm. There! She twisted the metal handle and felt the lock click. The door swung open so fast she barely had time to get her arm back out.

    Even in an emergency it was unsettling going into the driver's compartment. She felt out of bounds, like the time she'd had to enter the boys' bathroom at school to find her little brother.

12:35   She had hoped the controls would look like those of a car so she could figure out how to stop the train. No luck. There were four horizontal levers and two vertical ones, as well as a scattering of buttons and switches. Kelli-Anne could see that everything had once been labeled, but the labels had long since worn away.

    She would just have to try everything until she found the brake. What was the worst that could happen? She grabbed one of the vertical levers up high and yanked it.

12:00   *HONK!* The noise made her squeak with terror. She would have been horribly embarrassed if anybody else had been there to hear her.

"OK," she muttered. "That's the horn. Let's try this."

She yanked one of the horizontal levers to the left. It clicked through a number of slots and the engine rumbled with renewed vigor. The needle in one of the many dials rose up and up. Before Kelli-Anne realized what was happening the train had accelerated to a terrifying speed. The tracks blurred as they were sucked under the train and disappeared.

Kelli-Anne yanked the lever all the way back. The train didn't slow down, although it didn't seem to be accelerating as quickly. That lever must be connected to some sort of gear system.

11:00

With great fear she tried the lever beneath it. It clicked from the right side to the middle, which seemed to do nothing. When she tried to push it farther, the engine hacked and choked as though it had tried to swallow one of its gears. She hurriedly put the lever back where she found it.

10:50

Only two more levers to try. If neither one was the brake she would have to start trying the buttons and switches.

Then the train turned onto a long, straight run of track and she realized things were much worse than she had thought.

Something was on the tracks up ahead. At first it

just looked like a shadow, a black spot on the horizon. But as the train rocketed closer the obstruction became clearer—a car, parked sideways across the tracks.

10:00 Kelli-Anne screamed every swear word she knew. This was ridiculous! It was so *unfair*! Didn't she have enough problems? Why had this idiot chosen this particular day to park his dumb car on the stupid tracks?

She wrenched the horn lever and held it down.

HOOOOOOOOOOOOOONNNNK.

The car didn't move. Kelli-Anne grabbed one of the other mystery levers and hauled it sideways.

09:10 At last! The brakes screamed and Kelli-Anne was thrown forward out of her seat. She crashed into the control panel, hitting a whole bunch of switches. The alarms turned off and all the doors behind her opened with a hiss. She ignored all that and kept pulling hard on the brake.

08:30 The train was slowing down but not enough. If that car didn't get out of the way, it was going to get hit. Not only would that kill the driver, but Kelli-Anne would be in serious danger. There were no seatbelts anywhere. If the train derailed or tipped over, she could be pulverized against the walls.

The brakes kept shrieking. Kelli-Anne tugged at the horn again.

08:00 *HOOOONK! HOOOOOONNK!*

The car didn't move. And now she was so close that she could see there was no one in the driver's seat. A boy, no older than Kelli-Anne, was standing several feet away from it.

"What are you doing?" she howled, knowing the boy couldn't hear her.

The car wasn't going to move, and she couldn't stop the train in time. She was going to have to escape.

She pulled the elastic out of her hair and used the band to hold the brake in place. Then she ran out of the driver's compartment.

07:30

The side door was open, but it was facing a wall. If she jumped out that way, she would bounce back and be crushed under the wheels. Instead, she ripped the fire blanket off the wall, snatched up the extinguisher, and ran into the next carriage.

06:55

The packaged blanket was almost as heavy as the extinguisher. As she sprinted from one carriage to the next, and the next, and the next, she kept bumping into seats. The canister clanged each time it hit a stability pole.

By the time she reached the back of the train, she had no idea how much time she had left. How close was the car? Was it even still there?

06:30

With one adrenaline-fueled strike of the extinguisher, Kelli-Anne smashed through the back door. She reached through the hole, and then yanked the door open. The sudden noise was deafening. The wind ripped at her hair. She had slowed the train down as much as possible, but the tracks below still seemed to be sweeping away dangerously fast.

There was no time to hesitate. She held the fire blanket in front of her with both hands—

05:45 And jumped.

She was in midair when she heard the *smash* of the train crashing into the car. Despite the fact that she was several carriages away, the sound was like a deafening thunderclap. She rode the shockwave outward, clinging to the fire blanket as the railbed rushed up to meet her.

CRASH!

Even through the folded blanket the impact stung her knees and hands. The force shot upward into her torso, bending ribs and bouncing organs around. The leftover momentum threw her off the blanket and she tumbled backward onto the rocks and concrete sleepers of the railbed.

05:00 She lay still. The warm numbness all over her body told her that nasty bruises were forming. In a minute she would be in agony.

But she was alive.

She turned her aching head, wincing as the muscles in her neck stretched. The train had stopped a long, long way away. It must have plowed through the car like it was nothing.

But the angle was wrong. Kelli-Anne tilted her head some more. The train had come off the rails and was leaning against the wall of the narrow channel. If she had been on board—

"Hey, are you OK?"

She turned back to see a man approaching. He was a blur, but he was wearing blue. Like a police officer.

"Who are you?" she groaned.

03:50

He knelt beside her. "I was, uh, driving the train."

"No you weren't. *I* was driving the train." Then her eyes focused and she realized how much trouble she was in.

The man wasn't a cop. He was the conductor.

The one who had deliberately abandoned the train.

The one who had engineered the crash, and had presumably come here to pretend he was on board when it happened.

03:20

The one who now knew she was the only witness to his crime.

They stared at each either in frozen silence for a moment. The conductor looked as scared as she felt.

Then he snatched up a sharp rock from the

railbed and held it high, ready to smash her skull.

02:40 — As he brought it down, Kelli-Anne grabbed the fire blanket and pulled it over her like a shield. The rock thumped against it but didn't come through. Heart pounding, Kelli-Anne pushed the conductor off her and scrambled to her feet.

They circled one another for a moment, he holding the rock like a dagger, she clutching the blanket like a shield.

She had tried to ride the train without paying and had found herself hiding from transit police and smashing through doors with a fire extinguisher. The conductor had agreed to crash his train and had wound up threatening a teenage girl with a rock.

01:55 — In that moment, Kelli-Anne understood him completely.

"You don't have to do this," she said.

He lunged at her.

01:45 — She blocked the strike with the blanket but dropped it as she stumbled back. Her foot clunked against something and she fell over backward. The conductor ran at her, madness in his eyes, brandishing his rock like a Neanderthal.

Then Kelli-Anne realzed what she had tripped over.

The fire extinguisher.

She grabbed it, ripped the pin out, and squeezed

the handle. The conductor vanished in a freezing gray cloud of carbon dioxide. He screamed as Kelli-Anne scrambled backward out of the swirling mist. Then she stood up and fled toward the toppled train.

-00:55-

Sirens were wailing in the air. She looked up at the darkening sky, visible between the two walls of the channel. She could hear voices.

"Hey!" she screamed. "I'm down here! Hurry."

She shot a look back as the cloud of extinguisher fumes dissipated farther down the channel.

When they cleared, the conductor had gone. It was as if he'd never been there.

-00:20-

A head appeared from atop the channel. A face. A woman in a police hat and sunglasses.

"How did you get down there?" she demanded.

"I didn't have my rail pass," Kelli-Anne said, as though that explained everything. And then she fell to her knees and cried.

-00:00-

POISON

30:00 **"Y**ou've been poisoned," the tall man said.

Nassim was pretty sure he'd misheard that. He smiled politely. "Pardon me?"

The man didn't return the smile. The warmth had vanished from his luminous blue eyes. His lips pulled back to reveal a chipped tooth. He peeled off his latex gloves, revealing soft, pink hands with neatly clipped fingernails.

29:40 "You have thirty minutes to live," he said. "I'm a man of my word."

Fear flickered in Nassim's heart. "Aren't you here to fix the TV?"

"You're wasting time. Soon the nerve agent that you just drank will block the signals from your brain to your organs."

The bottle of ginger beer was cold in Nassim's hand. Suddenly he could see something through the tinted glass—a pill about the size of a maggot floating on the surface, fizzing.

He dropped the bottle. It hit the edge of the table

and smashed, sending sharp fragments skittering across the floorboards. The fluid spattered the wood and bubbled like acid.

29:10

"Soon you won't be able to walk," the poisoner continued. "After that you'll lose the ability to speak, and then to breathe. Unless I administer the antitoxin."

He put his briefcase on the table between them but didn't open it.

"Is this some kind of joke?" Nassim demanded.

"You're wasting time, Kim." The poisoner glanced at his plastic stopwatch. "In twenty-eight minutes and seven seconds—"

"My name isn't Kim."

28:00

"You will suffocate—unless I give you the anti-toxin."

He moved the briefcase so it was just out of Nassim's reach. It was made of dark gray plastic and looked airtight, as though the contents were fragile or had to be kept cool.

"Where is the bloodstone, Kim?"

27:40

"You've mixed me up with someone else," Nassim insisted. "I'm not Kim."

"Twenty seven minutes, thirty-one seconds."

There was no point screaming for help. Nassim's parents wouldn't be home for hours. His brother was away at band camp. The floor-to-ceiling windows were double-glazed and the brick walls were well-insulated. The neighbor's two-story townhouse was just on the other side of the hedge, but there was no way they would hear him.

26:35 Nassim felt like he was falling down a well. How had this happened?

A few minutes ago he was perfectly safe. He had just sunk into the leather couch with a ginger beer and a comic book—why do homework or wash his clothes when his parents weren't there to see it?—when the doorbell rang. He walked into the foyer to find this man on the doorstep, a clipboard in his hand and a cable company logo on the lanyard around his neck. He introduced himself as Daniel Leigh from CouchPotato and said he had come to repair the tuner so the missing channels would reappear on the TV.

26:00 Nassim wasn't aware of anything wrong with the television, but the man seemed very sure he had the right address. He said Nassim's mother had already paid for the service. Nassim might have called his mother to check this, but even when she remembered to take her phone with her—which was rare—she often left it switched off. So he shrugged and let the man in.

25:40 He should have asked more questions. He shouldn't have turned his back to pour the man a glass of water while he fiddled behind the television. He shouldn't have taken his eyes off his drink.

"Tell me where the bloodstone is, Kim," the poisoner said.

`25:00`

"I don't know who Kim is, I don't know who you are, and I don't know anything about any redstone!" Nassim's voice got higher and higher.

"Bloodstone. Do not test my resolve. After you saw my men come out of the bank, I ordered them to leave you on the train tracks. I ordered the train conductor to ram the car. I don't know how you survived, but you won't be so lucky twice."

It sounded like this "Kim" was having a very bad day. The poisoner would only be convinced he had the wrong person when Nassim died in front of him. But Nassim wasn't willing to wait that long. He wasn't going to die just because some jerk couldn't tell one kid from another.

He tried to grab the briefcase.

`24:00`

The poisoner slapped his hand out of the air. He did it so fast that his arms were back by his sides by the time Nassim felt the pain. It hurt so much he wondered if the bones in his hand were broken.

"That's not how this works," the poisoner told him. "You tell me where the bloodstone is, and then you get the antitoxin."

Nassim nursed his aching hand. "I don't know what you're talking about!"

"Don't lie to me. I have sources in the police department. I know they never found the bloodstone after the train crash. You're the only one who could have taken it. I saw you leave the police station and followed you here. There was no time to hide it anywhere else."

"I walked *past* the police station," Nassim insisted. "I was on my way home from school."

The poisoner grabbed him by the throat.

Nassim had no time to defend himself. A hand crushed his windpipe like a paper cup while another blocked his flailing strikes. He felt his face go purple as the poisoner lifted him out of the chair. The world started to go dark at the edges.

"This is what it will feel like," the poisoner hissed. "You'll be desperate for air but none will come. Your heart will keep beating for a while but the blood it pumps will slowly turn to acid. You'll be unable to scream or move, like a fly cocooned in a spider's web. They will find your body with an expression of utter terror on your face. It will give them nightmares for decades to come."

22:20 He let go. Nassim collapsed into the chair, hacking and wheezing. The poisoner waited, his hands neatly folded, until Nassim had recovered enough to speak.

// POISON //

The poisoner was willing to watch him die. Nassim could tell. He wouldn't even feel bad about it. Those were the eyes of a psychopath, someone who saw other people not even as animals but as furniture. Objects designed to serve his needs and his alone.

21:50

Convincing him that he wasn't Kim didn't seem like a good plan anymore. If Nassim succeeded, the poisoner might not even give him the antidote. He would probably just leave, taking the precious briefcase with him.

But what else could Nassim do?

"OK," he gasped.

"OK," the poisoner repeated.

"I'll take you to the bloodstone. It's upstairs."

The poisoner didn't look relieved. He didn't look anything. He had a face like a painting of an ancient Roman general—immobile, fearless, merciless.

"Lead the way," he said. "And tread carefully."

Somehow Nassim didn't think the poisoner was warning him about the stairs.

21:00

He rose to his feet and walked toward the spiral staircase. Glancing back, he saw that the poisoner had left the briefcase on the table. If Nassim could somehow incapacitate him upstairs, he could run back down and grab the antidote.

But he wasn't sure how to do that. There was

nothing in the house he could use as a weapon. Perhaps he could push the poisoner down the stairs?

As a child, Nassim had tripped his brother when they were playing in the park. It was supposed to be funny but his brother had cried and cried, leaving Nassim so twisted with guilt he felt like he might throw up. Since then he understood what people meant when they said someone didn't have "the stomach" for violence. Nassim didn't think his stomach would let him hurt a human being, even one as frightening as this man with the cold eyes and the fast hands.

He ascended the steps slowly, the banister smooth under his fingers. He had read somewhere that a spiral staircase was the only place in which it was polite to overtake on the inside, because the climb was steeper than at the outer edge.

19:10 The poisoner must have heard that theory too. He caught and overtook Nassim on the inside, probably not letting him get to the top first in case a weapon was up there. *I wish*, Nassim thought.

18:50 But nor did the poisoner get so far ahead that Nassim had the chance to run back down the stairs and grab the briefcase. Even if he was fast enough, how quickly could he take the antitoxin? Was it just a pill like the nerve agent? Or was it something too complicated to use quickly—like a syringe or eyedrops?

// POISON //

Nassim had never been good with needles. But he'd use one in a heartbeat if it would save his life.

"Hurry up," the poisoner said. "You don't have all day."

18:30

Nassim tramped up the stairs, terror curdling in his guts. He had only the vaguest wisp of a plan. He figured there were about eight ways it could go. In seven of them he would die.

"Which way?" the poisoner asked when Nassim reached the top.

Nassim pointed to his parents' bedroom.

The poisoner opened the door, glanced around, and beckoned. Nassim followed him in.

His parents' bedroom seemed bigger than it was. The full-length mirrors opposite the windows gave the illusion of a wide, airy space. An abstract painting hung behind the ornately carved four-poster bed.

If the poisoner was impressed or surprised by the luxury, he didn't show it. "Where?"

17:40

"Under the bed," Nassim said, without moving.

Just as he'd hoped, the poisoner didn't move either. "Go get it."

With fake reluctance Nassim dropped to his belly and wriggled under the bed.

There it was. His mother's phone, connected to the wall socket by a charging cable. He unlocked it, flicked it to silent, dialed 911, and hit the call button.

"What's taking so long?" the poisoner demanded.

"Just give me a minute."

With a whoosh that ruffled Nassim's hair, the mattress disappeared. He looked up to see the poisoner standing on the slats of the bed frame, glaring down at him. He managed to push the phone out of sight beneath a discarded pillowcase.

"Well? Where is it?"

Nassim could faintly hear a woman's voice on the phone: "Fire, ambulance, or police?"

He spoke loudly to cover the sound. "I don't understand," he said. "It was right here."

16:30

The poisoner grabbed the ceramic reading lamp on the bedside table and flung it. The lamp smashed through the window, sending a star-scape of glittering shards out into the daylight.

Nassim barely had time to wonder what he was doing before the poisoner grabbed him by the ankle and dragged him out from under the bed.

"Hey, wait, don't!" he cried.

16:10

The poisoner hauled him over to the window and pushed him out.

Nassim screamed as his legs dangled over the sickening drop. The poisoner was holding him by the collar of his shirt. If he let go, the paving stones below would break Nassim's legs, maybe even his spine. The broken glass and shards of the lamp could cut the arteries in his thighs and leave him bleeding to death.

"Perhaps I haven't been clear," the poisoner said.

Nassim tried to grab the window frame behind him, but he was being held too far out. Somewhere beneath the haze of fear it occurred to him that he should stop struggling, or else he might slip out of the poisoner's grip.

A stitch popped in his shirt. Then another.

"So let me make this very, very simple for you," the poisoner continued. "Give me the bloodstone, or you will die."

15:20

"If you let me fall, you'll never find it," Nassim panted.

"Wrong. You may have only fifteen minutes to live, but I have plenty of time. If I choose, I could spend the next three days tearing this house apart. Anyone else who arrives could be easily disposed of. The only reason you're still alive is that searching other people's homes is dull."

15:05

Nassim hoped the police were hearing all this. Another stitch burst in his collar. Soon he would fall.

"But it's not in the house!" he cried.

The poisoner hauled him back into the bedroom. The spikes of glass still attached to the window frame sliced Nassim's trousers to ribbons.

14:30

"Now we're getting somewhere," the poisoner said. "Is it in the backyard?"

Nassim had only meant to tell the truth—that he didn't have the bloodstone, had never had it, had never heard of it before now—but he saw an opportunity. If he could get outside, he could call for help and be heard. He might even be able to make a run for it, flag down a car, and get to a hospital.

Would fifteen minutes be long enough for them to test his blood, figure out what was in his system, and synthesize an antitoxin? He could only hope so.

14:15

"Yes," he said. "Buried by the gate."

The poisoner walked out the door and started to climb down the staircase. Nassim followed him. "I've told you where it is," he said. "Give me the antidote."

The poisoner had picked up the briefcase and was waiting at the back door. "After you dig up the bloodstone."

"I might not last that long. My legs hurt." This was true. A cold stiffness had spread from Nassim's toes to his knees, making it hard to walk. The world was starting to seem too bright. Part of him had been hoping this was all a prank and that there was no nerve agent in his body. Not anymore. He could feel

12:55 it dribbling into his cells and numbing them.

The poisoner seemed unmoved. "You should have thought of that before you stalled me," he said.

The doorbell rang.

They both turned to look toward the front foyer.

"Ignore it," the poisoner said.

The bell rang again. Someone thumped on the door itself and shouted, "Open up. Police."

By the time Nassim looked back at the poisoner, a gun was pointed at his face.

It was a small black thing, well-used but also well-polished, with a silencer screwed onto the barrel. Nassim wondered if the cops outside would hear the shot.

"Get rid of them," the poisoner said.

"How?"

"You'll think of something."

More banging. "Open up!"

"Coming!" Nassim shouted.

"If they don't leave, I will," the poisoner warned. "And I'll take the antitoxin with me. Your pupils are dilated. You don't have much time left."

Nassim ran around the corner to the foyer. He could see a silhouette behind the frosted glass door. Just one cop. Not enough to overpower the poisoner. Not enough to save him.

Nassim opened the door. "Can I help you, officer?"

The woman looked him up and down with bored brown eyes. Droplets of rain clustered at the corners of her cap. She wasn't much taller than Nassim. A gun was holstered on her hip, which didn't make him feel any safer. A patrol car was parked across the street, lights whirling. Nassim couldn't see if anyone was inside.

11:20

"Nassim al Parat?" she said.

Nassim wondered how she knew his name. "Yes," he said.

"I'm Constable Angela White," the cop said. "Is your mother home?"

"No." Someone must have traced the call to his mother's mobile account. "She and Dad are out. Has something happened?"

"We're not sure. Where did they say they were going?"

"To the shopping center. Dad needs a new raincoat."

11:00

"Uh-huh." White peered over his shoulder. "Can I come in?"

There was no time to get to a hospital now. Nassim's only hope was the antitoxin in the poisoner's briefcase.

He held the door a little more tightly. "Mom and Dad don't like people in their house when they're not here."

"It'll just be a minute."

10:45

"Do you have a warrant?"

White's eyebrows shot up under her hat.

"No," she said, "I don't."

Nassim shrugged helplessly. "I can give you Dad's number. You could call him and ask to speak to Mom."

"Why can't I call your mother?"

Uh-oh. "You could try. But her mobile is hardly ever switched on."

"I see."

White's face blurred. Nassim blinked, struggling to focus. He could feel a sheen of sweat clinging to his palms and forehead.

10:00

"Since I'm here," White said, "let me show you a picture."

She lifted up the papers on her clipboard and pulled a photo out from underneath. The picture showed a man walking out of a bank. He had a beard and wore a baseball cap and aviator sunglasses, but it was unquestionably the poisoner.

Was he one of the men this "Kim" had seen walking out of the bank? Or had he gone there first to check out the security?

"Have you seen this man?" White asked.

"No," Nassim said, too quickly.

09:25

White held the photo closer. "Are you sure?"

"No. I mean, yes. I'm sure."

"No problem. If you do see him, don't approach

him. Call us immediately, OK?"

"OK," Nassim said. "Sure."

"Let me show you one more picture."

09:00 Nassim gritted his teeth. He didn't have time for this.

The cop wrote something down on the back of the photograph and held it up. She had written: IS HE HERE?

Nassim froze. White clearly knew much more than she was letting on. He didn't want to lie to her, but he also didn't think she could help.

"Have you seen this person?" White asked.

08:10 Nassim had hesitated for too long. He had to tell the truth. He nodded.

White turned around and signaed to the patrol car across the street. "Well, never mind," she said loudly. "It was worth a try. As I said, if you do think you spot either of those people, give us a call. Before I go, can I come in for a glass of water?"

The poisoner would just shoot her, and maybe **07:45** Nassim too.

"No," Nassim said. "Sorry, but I've answered your questions. I think you should move on."

He closed the door before she had the chance to object.

He found the poisoner in exactly the same

position—feet firmly planted, gun up. Not even the expression on his face had changed.

07:30

"You called the cops," he said.

"No," Nassim said. "They had a picture. Someone must have seen you nearby."

"No one saw me. You did this."

Nassim wanted to scream. "I got rid of her, just like you asked! Give me the antidote!"

"No."

Nassim was a short kid. In primary school, other boys had often stolen his things—his library book, his pencil case, his glasses. The boy would pretend to offer the item back, but whenever Nassim reached for it the boy would laugh and hold it up high, just out of his reach.

07:00

He had learned that the easiest way to get the item back was to create a diversion. To start a sentence he had no intention of finishing.

"Listen." He made eye contact with the poisoner. "You have to—"

Then he grabbed for the gun.

The poisoner was quick but not quick enough. Nassim snatched the gun out of his grip. He had no idea how to use it, so instead he hurled it into the far corner of the room.

06:40

When the poisoner turned to chase it, Nassim

kicked the briefcase out of his hand.

06:00 The briefcase fell to the floor and popped open.

It was empty.

The poisoner was laughing. "Not bad, Kim. If things were different, I might hire you."

"Where's the antitoxin?" Nassim demanded.

"Not in there. Like I said, you'll get it when I have the bloodstone."

Nassim was about to reply when a jittery red dot appeared on the poisoner's forehead. The beam from a laser pointer.

05:40 It took Nassim a moment to put all the ramifications together.

There must be a police sniper outside the window.

And only the poisoner knew where the antitoxin to the poison was.

If he was killed—

"Down!" Nassim screamed. He crash-tackled the poisoner who stumbled back in surprise. A gunshot rang out. Glass smashed. A bullet whined through the air above Nassim's head and thunked into the wall, showering them both with plaster.

Wood splintered as someone kicked in the front door. Police boots thudded toward the living room.

The poisoner was already scrambling to the back **05:00** door. Another shot punched through the wall.

"Don't shoot!" Nassim cried. But the chances of being heard above the cacophony were minimal. He could hardly hear himself over the ringing in his ears.

No sooner had the poisoner disappeared through the back door than Constable White was standing over Nassim, decked out in body armor and surrounded by other cops.

"Which way did he go?" she demanded.

"Don't kill him!" Nassim tried to say, but his tongue was thick and heavy. His lips were stiff.

"Which way?"

`04:05`

Nassim couldn't speak anymore. He pointed at the back door.

Just as White was about to run after him, another cop burst in through the back door, dressed in full riot gear—jackboots, flak jacket, helmet.

"The backyard is clear," he said, his voice muffled by the helmet. "He got away."

`03:30`

No! Nassim tried to scream, but all that came up his throat was a groan. How could the poisoner have gotten away?

"Get back out there," White demanded. "Search the whole street!"

She ran toward the front door, leaving Nassim alone with the other cop.

"This isn't over, Kim," the cop said.

03:00 By the time Nassim realized that the cop was wearing street clothes under his flak jacket, he was gone. The back door swung shut.

Nassim tried to stand, but he couldn't. He crawled over to the door instead. When he pulled it open, he couldn't see the poisoner. Just an abandoned coat and some shoes on the back deck.

He dragged himself over and stuffed his hands into the pockets of the coat. He found a phone. Some keys. Ammunition.

There was no antitoxin.

Nassim's lungs felt increasingly tight. His brain throbbed as though it were too big for his head.

02:35 Maybe there had never been an antitoxin. Perhaps the poisoner had just dropped the nerve agent into Nassim's drink and used the empty briefcase to trick him into thinking he could save himself.

And yet . . .

02:00 *I'm a man of my word.*

It seemed foolish to trust a killer. But had the poisoner ever actually said the antitoxin was in the briefcase? Nassim tried to think back. No. He had merely let Nassim assume that.

So if there was an antitoxin, and it wasn't in the briefcase or the pockets of the poisoner's coat, where could it be?

`01:40`

Nassim tried to think back to when the poisoner had first arrived at the house, when he was still pretending to be a TV repairman—

And suddenly he had it.

He hauled his numb body back into the house. His knees wouldn't bend. He felt as helpless as a newborn baby.

He crawled over to the television, spilled ginger beer soaking his shirt and torn trousers. The television was still slightly crooked from when the poisoner had been fiddling with it.

`01:15`

Nassim dragged himself around behind it. He rolled sideways far enough to see the back of the TV—

There it was. An inhaler, like the kind he had for his asthma, taped to the plastic among the cables.

`00:55`

Nassim reached up with a trembling arm. It took him three attempts to grab the inhaler. By the time he eventually peeled it off the back of the TV, he couldn't breathe anymore.

He tried to pop the cap off the inhaler but his fingers wouldn't obey him. His whole body was shutting down. The world was a blur. He could hardly see what he was doing.

I'm too late, he thought. *It's over.*

Then Constable White walked in and saw Nassim

sprawled out on the floor.

"Nassim?" she said. "Are you OK?"

Nassim couldn't reply. He was paralyzed.

White ran over. She looked at the inhaler in his hand. "What's this?" she asked.

Come on! Nassim thought. *Figure it out!*

`00:10` White didn't waste any more time asking questions. She popped the cap off the inhaler and jammed it between Nassim's lips.

The last thing Nassim heard before he blacked out

`00:00` was a soft, beautiful hiss.

SPACE RACE

Pop.

The sound was barely audible over the humming instruments.

"What was that?" Jessie Pavel asked.

Commander Washington looked over at her. "What was what?"

"It sounded like this." Jessie made a popping noise with her lips.

"We've just tilted seven degrees. Part of the spaceship that was in the shade is now in the sun. You may have heard the hull expanding."

"It didn't do that last time we changed course."

Washington checked the luminous screen. "We've got exactly one atmosphere of air pressure. Temperature 18.2—normal. O_2 isn't dropping, CO_2 isn't rising. Fuel level steady, solar cells charged. Speed unchanged—5,000 miles per hour. Whatever you heard, it can wait."

Washington was a big man with a bald patch and a heavy brow. His expression was neutral. No sign

`30:00`

`29:40`

`29:10`

that he resented having to look after her. But Jessie knew he did.

"I ran twelve miles every day for eight years," she had overheard him telling a mechanic. "I ate nothing but brown rice, lentils, and boiled chicken. I studied astrophysics, chemistry, and advanced mathematics. And now this girl waltzes in, with barely three months of training, thinking she can be an astronaut?"

28:50

I can, Jessie wanted to say. *StarTours tested every kid in the country to find the perfect candidate. Me.*

But arguing wouldn't convince him. It would only make the journey awkward. Icarus was a two-compartment shuttle. No room to avoid each other. So Jessie walked quietly away, leaving the astronaut she admired most to trash her reputation in peace.

She understood Washington's bitterness. Soon she would be the youngest person to ever visit the Genesis III Space Station. StarTours would make a fortune if they could prove that space travel was safe for children, so they had sent her on a huge promotional tour. Right now, hundreds of people were watching interviews with her down on Earth. Washington, the one who had to do most of the actual work, was rarely mentioned.

28:30

Down on Earth. It was a strange thought. They were only 100 miles up—half the distance from her house to the StarTours training base—but she'd never felt so far from home.

"You should suit up, Pavel," Washington said. "We'll be docking with the Genesis III in twenty minutes, assuming there's no space junk."

Jessie floated through the control room to the tiny circular window and peered out. Floating didn't feel like floating—it felt like falling. But she had gotten used to the nausea. In training, one of her tasks had been to assemble a wooden puzzle inside a jet as it plummeted from the upper atmosphere toward the ground. The pieces kept bouncing off her fingers and drifting away, but at least she kept her breakfast down. The other astronauts called this jet "the vomit comet."

Through three thick panes of transparent polymer she could see Earth, massive and blue above them. But she couldn't see the space station.

"It's on the other side of the world at the moment," Washington said, as if reading her mind. "But it'll be visible soon. It does a full circle—"

"Every ten minutes. I know." Jessie pushed off the window and flew through the air. It still amazed her that Genesis III could travel around the whole world— more than 25,500 miles—in the time it took her to walk to her local supermarket.

"*Eleven* minutes," Washington corrected. "Get that suit on."

Jessie was already wearing her space suit, which somehow felt heavy even in zero-gravity. But her helmet was fixed to the wall by a velcro strip. Once she attached it to her suit and engaged the seal, it would take a couple of minutes for the pressure to equalize.

27:05

She grabbed the helmet and pulled.

It wouldn't come off the wall.

Jessie frowned. The velcro shouldn't be that strong. And it looked like the visor, not the adhesive strip, was stuck to the wall.

Another helmet hung next to it, but Washington would need that one. Jessie bent down and peered up through the neck of the stuck helmet—

And saw stars.

She gasped. "Commander!"

26:25

"Listening." Washington was tapping some numbers into a touchscreen.

Jessie's heartbeat was deafening in her ears. "Something's punctured the hull!"

Washington's head swiveled around immediately. "That's impossible. The atmospheric pressure—"

26:10

"This helmet is plugging the leak," Jessie said. "The negative pressure must have sucked it there. I don't know how long the seal will hold."

Now that she was closer, she could hear a soft hissing, like a venomous snake. They were losing air.

Washington unbuckled his five-point harness. "Put the other helmet on."

"What about you?"

"Just do it."

Jessie grabbed the other helmet and pulled it on. The clamps snapped down onto her suit. Before launch she had cut her hair short so it didn't get tangled in the mechanism. Her ears popped as the pressure began to equalise.

Washington launched himself over. He took a look up into the neck of the stuck helmet and swore. He wrenched a patch kit out of a pocket on his space suit.

"That was designed to repair holes in a suit," Jessie said. "Not the ship."

`25:00`

The microphone in his collar picked up his voice and transmitted it to the speakers in Jessie's helmet: "I know. It'll buy us some time. Get into the storage compartment. Close the door behind you."

"You don't have a helmet. I should fix the leak."

"You don't have the training." Washington was already squeezing resin out of a tube, fixing the helmet to the wall. "Get in there. That's an order!"

Jessie launched off the hull toward the storage compartment.

`24:40`

She almost made it.

There was a dull rip she heard even through her

helmet, and then silence. Sound waves were made of variations in air pressure—no air meant no noise. Jessie found herself falling backward. Pens, water bottles, and other assorted debris hurtled past her, sucked toward the breach. Warning lights were flashing all over the control room, but she couldn't hear any of the alarms. All she could hear was her own terrified breaths bouncing around the inside of her helmet.

As she spun, she got a look at what she was falling toward. A massive rip in the hull, stars glimmering on the other side. Washington's helmet was hurtling down to Earth.

Washington himself was tangled in one of the storage nets attached to the wall. His eyes bulged, motionless, unseeing.

"Commander!" Jessie cried.

No response. Even if Washington had survived the sudden loss of oxygen and exposure to sub-zero temperatures, he wouldn't have been able to hear her without his helmet.

23:10 Jessie flailed about, grasping for something, anything. Her gloved hands found one of the harness straps from Washington's chair. She yanked hard on it, stopping her descent. Now that all the air was gone, she wasn't being sucked toward the hole in the hull anymore.

Jessie pushed off the chair. When she hit the wall, she grabbed the support struts and crawled over to Washington's body.

The stars outside were spinning. Even with her vomit-comet training it was hard not to feel sick. She squeezed Washington's outstretched hand. No reaction.

She untangled him from the net and pushed him toward the storage compartment. His lifeless body drifted in the vacuum until it hit the door. Jessie jumped after him, floating through the control room just in time to stop Washington from bouncing out of reach. She clipped his belt to hers so that he didn't float away.

`21:50`

If she opened the compartment door now, all the air would explode out, blasting her and Washington out through the breach into space. She prodded the touch-screen next to the door and triggered a decompression.

She waited for twelve agonizing seconds while all the air was sucked out of the storage compartment and sealed in tanks. As soon as the pressure gauge hit zero, she wrenched the door open and dragged Washington inside.

`21:20`

Everything on the ship was cramped, but the storage compartment was even more so. Two massive gas tanks marked O_2 and N dominated the room, leaving just enough space for a crate of MREs, or Meals Ready to Eat.

20:00 Jessie slammed the door shut. There was a touch-screen in here too. She jabbed it until she found the setting to pour the air back in. When the storage compartment reached 0.8 atmospheres of pressure, she detached her helmet.

Her ears popped and the cold hit her like an alpine river. She ignored it. "Commander Washington," she shouted. "Can you hear me?"

Washington didn't respond. He simply floated like a mannequin filled with helium.

19:30 Jessie ripped off her glove and pressed her fingers to his throat, searching for a pulse. She had to hold one hand behind his head to stop him from floating away.

Thump, thump. Thump, thump.

A pulse!

She pulled Washington toward the door and positioned his face over the touchscreen. A fog of condensation appeared on the glass. He was breathing.

19:05 Jessie almost wept with relief. Washington wasn't dead. Unconscious, yes—maybe even in a coma—but his lungs and heart were working. Perhaps running twelves miles every day for eight years and eating only rice, lentils, and chicken really could make someone invincible.

(174)

"You're tough, I'll give you that." She wiped her eyes and held up her hand. "High five."

18:20

Washington didn't respond.

The radio in Jessie's suit was only designed to communicate with people up to half a mile away. But the craft itself could broadcast much farther. Jessie prodded the touchscreen and opened a channel.

"Atlas, this is Icarus," she said. "Atlas, this is Icarus. Come in, over," she said.

A heart-stopping delay as the signal traveled down to Earth. And then:

"We read you, Icarus." A female voice. "What's your status?"

17:50

"There's a breach in the hull," Jessie said. "The control room is depressurized. Commander Washington and I are in the storage compartment. I'm OK, but he's unconscious."

To her credit, Atlas didn't sound panicked. "What are his vital signs?"

"He's breathing and he has a pulse, but he's not responding to anything I say."

17:20

"What about the breach in the hull? Are you able to patch it?"

Jessie peered through the small window above the doorhandle. "I don't think so," Jessie said. "It's at least six feet long and three feet wide."

"Oh. Copy that, Icarus. Stand by for instructions."

Silence fell. Jessie put her palm on Washington's forehead. His skin was no longer freezing. She hoped that meant he was recovering, but the sooner he got medical help, the better.

16:30

"This is Atlas calling Icarus."

"Uh, go ahead."

"I've got some bad news," Atlas said.

"More?" Jessie demanded. "Seriously?"

"The decompression has knocked you out of orbit."

"I'm going to crash?" Jessie felt dizzy.

"No. The escaping air pushed Icarus in the opposite direction. You're headed away from Earth. You need to change course, or else you'll find yourself in deep space where we can't help you."

"OK. How do I do that?"

"Are the controls intact?" the woman asked.

Jessie peered through the window. The instrument panel had all the usual lights on—plus some extras warning about the decompression.

"I think so," she said. "But I can't get to them. The breach is in the control room. I can't pressurize it."

"You'll have to fly Icarus wearing your spacesuit," Atlas said. "You passed your flight training, right?"

"Yes, but I can't open the door. All the air will escape from the storage compartment."

"You'll have to depressurize the compartment first."

"I can't! Commander Washington will suffocate."

"He doesn't have a flight suit?"

"Suit, yes," Jessie said. "Helmet, no. It was sucked out into space."

15:45

"Stand by."

There was a longer silence this time—or maybe it seemed longer because Jessie was dreading the answer.

One helmet. Two astronauts. One with years more training than the other.

What if Atlas told Jessie to give away her helmet? What if someone decided Washington's life was more important than hers?

She told herself that wouldn't happen. Washington couldn't fly the ship while he was unconscious. But she found herself chewing her nails, a habit she'd thought she had broken.

"Icarus, come in."

"I'm here," Jessie said warily.

"We've talked to the crew of Genesis. We think we have a plan."

15:05

Relief washed through her. A plan!

"You're not far off course," Atlas continued. "Your new trajectory will bring you within forty-five feet of

Genesis. When it comes past, a member of the crew is going to jump off the hull, land on Icarus, climb in through the breach, and pilot your craft to safety."

Jessie boggled at the screen. "What if he misses?"

"Her name is Racine. She's the best we have—she won't miss."

"But what if she does?"

"She'll be tethered to Genesis and won't unhook unless she lands on Icarus successfully. If she were to miss, she'd be able to reel herself back in. But you guys would be in serious trouble. By the time Genesis came around again, you'd be out of reach."

Fear gnawed at Jessie's stomach. "Thanks for being honest with me."

"She won't miss," Atlas said again.

"What can I do?"

"Just sit tight. She should be landing on your hull in about two minutes."

"Copy that."

Jessie checked Washington's pulse again. It would be awful if he died while they were waiting to be rescued. But his heartbeat was steady. His breaths were now audible—no need to hold his face up to the glass. Jessie wasn't a doctor but she thought his chances were good.

She pressed her face against the window. She

thought she could see a spot in the black void beyond the breach. At first it was no bigger than the spinning vortex of stars around it. But soon it got bigger and bigger until she could make out details. Two grids of solar panels, sixteen in all, on either side of a box-shaped chassis. Genesis, coming in fast.

"Icarus." The voice was fuzzy. "We . . . problem."

"What's going on?"

". . . Telescope . . . looks . . . solar flare."

Jessie's blood ran cold. A solar flare—a sudden explosion on the sun's surface—was every astronaut's nightmare. It could disrupt radio communications, disable electronics and knock spacecraft out of orbit. And worse, any astronaut who was outside their ship when it happened would be fried.

`13:00`

"Tell Racine not to jump!" Jessie cried, although Atlas was probably already doing that. "Tell her not to—"

Outside the window there was a moment of brightness, just like the flash of a camera. Everything in the control room sparkled for a split-second. If the breach in the hull had been facing the sun, Jessie would have been blinded, and perhaps burned.

`12:50`

Then the flare was over. All the lights in the ship sputtered and went dark, fried by the distant explosion.

Jessie watched as Genesis swept past. No one

jumped off the hull. Racine must have gotten the message in time . . .

But that meant no help was coming. Icarus would spin farther and farther away from Earth, with Jessie and Washington trapped inside.

11:50 It took a minute for the electronics to reset themselves. Some of the lights came on. Others didn't.

The radio crackled. "Sorry, Icarus. Racine couldn't do the jump. She would have been burnt to a crisp."

"Can they try again?" Jessie asked. "The next time they come around?"

"The tether is only sixty-five feet long," Atlas said. "You'll be ninety feet away from Genesis next time it passes you."

Jessie tried not to sound desperate. "Can they change course?"

"It's a space station, not a shuttle. They can slow down or speed up, but they can't turn."

So we're going to die, Jessie thought. "Is there anything else we can try?"

There was a pause. Then, "Stand by."

It seemed unlikely. The jump had been their last chance. Jessie wondered how long she and Washington would survive before the oxygen ran out, or the food, or the water, or the heat.

Her parents would be left with no corpse to bury.

But she would at least have the chance to say goodbye, right? Before they were out of radio range?

Tears stung her eyes. When she blinked, the droplets floated away toward the wall.

"Icarus."

11:00

"I'm here." Jessie tried to keep her voice steady.

"You'll need to put on the space suit and steer the ship back into orbit," Atlas said. "There's no other way."

"What about Commander Washington?"

Atlas said nothing.

"I can't tell him to hold his breath," Jessie said. "He's unconscious. The depressurization will kill him."

"He knew the risks."

Jessie looked at Washington's body floating helplessly in the air.

10:40

"It's because I'm a kid, isn't it?" she demanded. "No one will care about a dead astronaut who's a grown man. But if a kid dies, StarTours will have to cancel the whole program."

"We care plenty," Atlas snapped. "But Washington's mission—which he willingly signed up for—was to protect you at all costs."

Jessie ran her hands through her hair. Could she really sacrifice Washington's life to save her own?

"No," she said.

"There isn't any other way," Atlas said.

"Yes there is." Jessie put her helmet over Washington's head and attached it to his suit. She heard a faint hiss from inside as it pressurised. "Tell the astronaut to get ready for a second jump."

"The tether isn't long enough. And at this distance, she's much more likely to miss, so she can't jump without it."

"She doesn't need to come to us," Jessie said. "We're going to meet her halfway."

There was a small medical bay in the storage room. Some bandages, scissors, antibacterial cream—and an oxygen canister. Jessie wound a roll of duct tape around her body, fixing the canister to her back.

08:10 "Are you talking about jumping?" Atlas demanded.

Jessie pulled a plastic breathing mask over her nose and mouth and taped up the valves so the air wouldn't escape.

"You can't jump," Atlas said. "You don't have a spare helmet. Or a tether."

The mask muffled Jessie's voice. "Feel free to fly up here and stop me."

06:20 A bag tied to the wall contained ear plugs and goggles. The lenses were designed to keep out most of the light so the crew could sleep. Jessie pulled the goggles on—Washington's eyeballs hadn't exploded in the vacuum, but that didn't mean hers wouldn't.

She licked the ear plugs for a better seal and jammed them into her ears, wincing at the slimy texture. Her eyes, lungs, and eardrums were all protected. Nothing she could do about the cold. She would just have to hope that she stayed conscious long enough to make the jump.

`05:00`

She clipped Washington's belt to her own again.

"If this works, you owe me big time," she told him.

No response. A pity.

Jessie squinted out the window. It was hard to tell with the dark goggles, but was that Genesis coming around again already?

"Is Racine ready to jump?" she asked.

"Jessie, I am ordering you not to do this."

"I didn't quite catch that, Atlas," Jessie said. "Commander Washington and I will make the jump as soon as Genesis comes into view. Will Racine be ready to catch us?"

`03:40`

A long pause. Then: "She says she will. She's as crazy as you are. Genesis is slowing down so you don't get killed on impact."

`03:00`

Jessie put her hand on the doorhandle. No sign of unusual solar activity, space junk, or any other hazards—except that freezing, hungry vacuum, waiting to pull her brains out through her eye sockets.

There it was—a white dot appearing from behind

Earth's horizon.

She should have asked Atlas to give a message to her parents in case she didn't make it. Too late now.

She turned the handle.

02:20 The air exploded out of the room and the cold rushed in like a tsunami. Jessie's skin turned to ice. It was somehow like being burned. She could feel the veins standing out all over her body.

She'd made a terrible mistake. This was impossible.

But it was too late to change her mind.

She hauled Washington out the door into the control room. The breach seemed even more terrifying now that there was no protective helmet between her and it. The unforgiving blackness of outer space yawned. Flecks of the shredded hull floated around her like dust in an ancient library. Jessie pushed through it toward the breach.

02:00 Genesis was getting bigger. Jessie tried not to think about how fast it was going, and what she was about to do—jump onto it carrying a man who was at least twice her weight.

She had no tether. If she missed Racine, she and Washington would drift away into space. She would freeze to death, and Washington would eventually suffocate in his sleep.

Fortunately the icy sizzling all over her skin was very distracting. The vacuum was pulling at her, stretching her in every direction at once. It was like a vampire, desperate to pull the blood out of her body. **01:50**

Jessie crawled out through the breach into the void of space and was hit with a wave of vertigo. The ship was still spinning—right now Earth was a massive gray-blue ball above her, but it was sweeping slowly around so that soon it would be below. The first time Jessie went camping she had been struck by how bright the stars were away from the smog of the city, but that was nothing compared to this. The stars—suns, she reminded herself, each hotter than the inside of a volcano—were almost painfully bright, even through the goggles. **01:25**

The space station was a looming behemoth now. She could see Racine clinging to the hull, ready to leap. If Jessie didn't jump toward Genesis now she would miss her chance.

She crouched low, holding Washington in her arms so that his mass didn't interfere with her trajectory . . .

And launched herself into space. **01:05**

As soon as her feet left the hull the terror became too big to ignore. What if she had misjudged the angle? She could drift away into the endless void until her body crash-landed on a distant moon, got sucked into a black hole, and squished or was incinerated inside a distant star.

But Racine had angled her jump perfectly. She was hurtling toward Jessie, both arms outstretched, the tether trailing behind her like a yellow ribbon. She was already close enough that Jessie could see her intense eyes behind the visor of her helmet.

`00:50` *Crash!* The impact was completely silent but Jessie felt it in every joint. Racine's arms encircled her. The tether went taut and swung them outward like a tennis ball around a totem pole, and suddenly all three astronauts were being dragged after Genesis.

The tether got shorter. Someone was reeling them in. Jessie tried to examine the approaching airlock, but her eyes wouldn't focus. The sun must have gone behind the Earth because it was getting darker, and

`00:00` darker, and . . .

⚡

"Ghuh!" Jessie awoke with a gasp.

She wasn't in space. She was somewhere bright and warm. Her goggles had gone and a blanket was tangled around her body. Had it all been a dream?

But she was still wearing an oxygen mask. She had that constantly-falling zero-gravity sensation.

She must be in a spaceship—Genesis.

She had made it.

She turned her head and moaned. Her whole body felt like one big bruise. Looking down she saw that her skin had a purplish hue.

Commander Washington hung in the air next to her. A tube led from a machine to a needle inside his elbow, dripping a transparent fluid into his bloodstream.

It took him a moment to notice that she was awake.

"Jessie," he said. He had never called her by her first name before. "Can you hear me?"

She tried to nod, but her neck was stiff. Washington seemed to register the movement.

"I owe you one," he said. "You're a great kid."

"Wrong," Jessie croaked. "I'm a great *astronaut*."

ACKNOWLEDGMENTS

Huge thanks to the team at Sterling Publishing for embracing the Countdown to Disaster series and updating it for a North American audience. Thank you to the army of booksellers, librarians, teachers, and readers who made it such a success in Australia. Thanks to Clare Forster, Angie Masters, Tiffany Malins, Claire Pretyman, Benjamin Stevenson, Kate Wenban, and everyone else who worked on the book. Thanks to Happening Films, The Pulse Originals, and the cast and crew of the *30 Minutes of Danger* film. And as always, thanks to my family and friends for your encouragement and indulgence.

Photo credit © Ash Peak, 2013

JACK HEATH was born in 1986 and published his first novel as a teenager. He is now the award-winning author of fourteen books for young people. He lives in Canberra with his wife, their son, and their dog.